HIS *Bunny* KICKS *Sass*

Published by Dawn Sullivan

Cover Design: Tracie Douglas with Dark Water Covers

Language: English

HIS BUNNY KICKS SASS

Emery Ericksen fled her herd, intent on escaping an arranged marriage to an abusive alpha. Ending up in a small town, she works as a waitress at the Lyon's Den, saving up as much money as possible so that she can move on before she winds up on one of the local felines' dinner menu. She managed to stay under the radar, not attracting too much attention, until he walked into the bar. A possessive bear with a gruff attitude, who wanted to throw her over his shoulder, take her back to his cave, and do delicious things to her. What was fate thinking giving her a bear for a mate, anyway?

After the death of his parents, Knox Channing moved his family to the small town of Moonstone where they could build a new life. He loves his family, his ranch, and his solitude-in that order. If he had his way, he would never leave the peace and quiet of his home. All that changes when he catches her scent. After years of being alone, he finally found his mate. She was beautiful, curvy as hell, and... a bunny?

Sure there is no chance of a future with Knox, Emery believes she must stick to her original plan, hopping town as soon as possible. Even if Knox can stop her from running, will he be able to keep her safe from her past when it catches up with her?

For all my readers out there who love a little sass with their growl...this series is for you!

ACKNOWLEDGMENTS

Tracie Douglas with Dark Water Covers- The cover you designed for His Bunny Kicks Sass is absolutely gorgeous! I can't wait to see what you do with the rest in this series. Thank you!

My beta readers- You all seriously ROCK! Thank you for all that you do for me!

My readers- I wouldn't be where I am today without all of your support. Thank you, from the bottom of my heart.

ONE

The wind whipped past her as she ran full speed ahead, the loud voices behind her getting closer and closer. She was only a mile away from where she was supposed to meet the person who was going to help her escape the madness she'd found herself in these past few months, but the way it was looking, she might not make it that far.

"You can't run from us, Princess!"

Wanna bet? She thought, as she pushed harder, biting her lip so she wouldn't cry out when a large tree branch appeared out of nowhere, smacking her in the forehead. Groaning, she stopped and caught her balance, before taking off again. It hurt like a bitch, and she couldn't stop the tears that slipped out, rolling down her cheeks, as she jumped over the log in front of her and picked up more speed. She could smell blood and knew the branch had done some damage, but she ignored it, along with the pain that was now vibrating through her skull. She had to get away. This was her only chance. If they caught her, she would have to suffer the consequences, and there was a very good possibility she would not survive.

She was so close to her destination that she could practically taste it, when all of a sudden she heard the sound of running footsteps right behind her. Someone was quickly closing the distance between them. Inhaling deeply, she bit out a curse when she recognized Dryden's scent, hating the enforcer for turning against her. She should have expected it, though. It was what they all did after her father passed away, but he'd held out the longest. Her heart jumped in her chest when she glanced back and saw how close he was. The bastard was fast.

"The alpha of the Blackstone herd wants you. You were promised to him by your brother. You know Alpha Ramsey is very powerful, Princess, and always gets what he wants!" Dryden growled, reaching out and snagging hold of the hood of her sweatshirt.

"Not this time, asshole," she snarled. She would not go back there. Her brother may have chosen the scary, shady as hell alpha to become her mate, but he wasn't her choice. She had vowed many years ago to wait for her fated mate, and that wasn't going to change just because some douche canoe wanted to claim what wasn't his.

Willing her animal to rise to the surface, she extended her claws and sliced through the front of her sweatshirt, yanking her arms from the sleeves when Dryden pulled on it, leaving her in just a thin tee-shirt that had seen better days. After being held prisoner for weeks, punishment for her refusal to accept the alpha, more than just her clothing had suffered. She was weak from lack of food and water, and her body was covered in bruises from where her brother, Samson, tried to force her compliance.

What hurt the most was that no one in her family or herd stepped up to help her. Not her mother, Lela, nor her other two brothers, Frederick and Hamilton. After the death of their father, Samson became the alpha of their herd, and no one crossed him. Not anyone who lived to talk about it, anyway.

Except for one person. Someone she never imagined would have reached out to her in her time of need, even if it was in the dark quiet of the night where no one else would know. She would forever be grateful to that person for giving her this chance to escape. And, she was so close to making it happen. She could hear the sound of the rushing water from the waterfalls in the distance. If she could just get to them, she would be free. Either that, or she would be dead.

"Dammit! Stop this! You are only going to piss them both off!"

Like she cared if dickhead Ramsey or her jerk of a brother were mad at her. All Ramsey wanted to do was get in her pants, and there was no way in hell she was going to let that happen. He wasn't getting his wrinkled up old pudwacker near her. And, her brother? He was greedy, plain and simple. He was only in it for the money. It was all he cared about.

"Princess, wait! You are going to get yourself killed!"

The falls came into sight in front of her, and soon she skidded to a stop at the edge of the cliff. It was a long drop, one she wasn't looking forward to making, but the alternative was worse. Jump into the dark, stormy depths below, or go back and spread her legs for Ramsey. In her mind, there was only one choice to make. Looking back at Dryden, she spat, "I would rather die than mate with that pompous ass!"

"He would be good to you," Dryden promised, but she could smell the rancid stench of his lies even though he was several feet away from her. There was also the scent of fear, and she knew it was because if she got away, it was his ass on the line.

"We both know that's not true," she ground out, shaking her head slowly. "Tell my family... never mind, don't tell them anything." They were the ones who put her in this situation in the first place. They didn't deserve any last words from her.

"Princess!"

Turning from him, she took a deep breath, and then closed her eyes and stepped off the ledge. The sound of Dryden shouting was immediately muffled when she hit the ice-cold water below just a few moments later. It tugged on her, dragging her down deep, not wanting to let her go. She swallowed a mouth full of the murky water, gagging as she kicked hard, struggling to get back to the surface. Her head barely broke the top, and then she was under again, the water pushing her back down, wanting to take her last breath as its own.

You must fight.

The voice slid into her mind, but it sounded distant, far away. Who was it? Was it real, or just a figment of her imagination? Was she dreaming? Had the wild, raging water won already?

I can't, she whispered, coughing when water began

to stream into her lungs. She was so tired of fighting. She just wanted to close her eyes and go to sleep. She was alone and terrified. She had just jumped off a cliff into freezing water to escape her family; the people who were supposed to love her and be there for her, but instead had tried to sell her to the highest bidder. They were all a bunch of lowdown weasels, but they were all she knew.

Stop that. You may not know me now, but you will. I'm here to help you, and I promise, I won't leave you. You have a bigger purpose, Princess. You have a future waiting for you. Fight for it!

Her limbs felt heavy, and she was so tired, but the voice in her head would not stop. It kept pushing at her until she finally growled low in her throat and started kicking harder. Using both her arms and legs, she fought her way back to the top, taking in a huge lungful of the crisp night air as soon her head broke the surface to ease the pain in her chest.

I'm over here! Look! When she didn't respond, the woman yelled, *Look, dammit!*

She was so cold, but she squinted through the shadows of the night, her eyes widening when they landed on the figure in the dark cloak standing on the riverbank not far from her. The moon hid behind the clouds above, but she was able to catch a glimpse of the woman's pale features surrounded by long, auburn hair when she slipped the hood back.

That's it! Come to me, the woman ordered. *Just a little bit further, and you will be home free!*

Slowly, she started to swim, closing the distance between herself and the other woman. She was almost there, when she heard a loud crack, and she gasped when the branch from an overhanging tree fell into the water in front of her.

"Grab onto it!" she ordered, stepping into the water and grasping the other end. "Jesus, help me out some, Princess," the woman grunted, as she hauled her up onto the embankment.

Yelling could be heard in the background, and she raised her weary head to glance behind her and up to the top of the cliff, where several people looked over the side. One man stood out in front of the other, and through the light of the moon, she could see the hatred on his face when he raised his fist and hollered, "You will not get away from me that easily, Princess! You are mine! I'm coming for you!"

"Not Princess anymore," she gasped, her eyes going back to the other woman as a deep shudder racked her body.

"No, you aren't."

"What's your name?" she rasped, needing to know who her rescuer was. The woman had put a lot on the line for her, and she would never forget it.

"I'm Aurora, and I have come to take you to your new life, Emery."

Emery, she thought, rising slowly to her feet, swaying back and forth until Aurora slipped an arm around her waist. "I like it," she whispered, as they began to move toward the dirt road where she could see the outline of a car through the trees. "Where are we going?"

"A small town called Moonstone. You'll be safe there."

6

Safe. That was one word she hadn't known for a long time. One she didn't trust. "Thank you," she murmured, stumbling over a rock, a low moan slipping out as pain engulfed her head.

"It's okay, we're almost there."

She leaned heavily on Aurora the rest of the way, her body shaking with chills. "I'm soooo coldddd."

Aurora helped her into the car and left her, returning soon with a blanket. Wrapping it around her shoulders, she smiled gently, "Let's get going, Emery. It's time to start over and lead the life you were meant to live."

Her head hurt, her body ached, and it felt as if she were on fire. A soft whimper left her throat as she struggled to open her eyes. She had never felt so miserable in her life.

"Hush, sweet girl," a low voice murmured, and she winced when something cool and wet was pressed against her forehead. "It's going to be all right. You are fighting a fever and sickness from your fall into the water."

"Cold," she whispered, shaking as chills wracked her body. Her teeth began to chatter, and she cried out when she accidentally bit her tongue.

"You will feel better soon, Emery," someone else said quietly. "We just need to get you well enough to shift. That will help a lot."

She knew that voice, although she couldn't put a face to it, but who was Emery? Her brow furrowed as she struggled to recall where she'd heard that name before.

"Emery?" she gasped, finally managing to pry her eyes open just enough to see through tiny slits.

"That's your name now, remember?"

Clearing her throat, she licked her dry lips before rasping, "Everything's foggy."

"It's okay, child," the old woman next to her crooned. Sliding an arm under her, the woman helped raise her up slightly, and then slipped a teaspoon of something into her mouth.

"What is that?" Emery gagged, weakly grasping the hand that held the spoon. It was bitter, with a nasty taste, and she immediately pulled back, trying to get away from it.

"It's just something to help you rest, Emery," the woman said, laying her back down and gently running a hand over her hair. "Sleep now. When you awake, you should feel well enough to shift. After that, you and Aurora can talk."

Aurora. She knew that name. Slowly turning her head, she caught the silhouette of a woman sitting next to a brick fireplace on the other side of the room. Her head was bowed, and her long hair covered most of her face. Emery could see that her lips were moving slightly, but no sound could be heard.

"I remember you," she whispered, reaching toward the woman, before letting her arm fall weakly beside her. She was exhausted, and hard as she tried, she just couldn't seem to stay awake. "You helped me." A soft sigh slipped from her lips, and her eyes slid shut as she slipped into unconsciousness.

She was unaware of the shadowed glance exchanged

by Aurora and the old woman that spoke of what was to come.

"Will she make it, Grandmother?"

"Only time will tell. The road ahead will be a hard one, granddaughter. If she chooses the right path, she will know a happiness like no other."

"And if she doesn't?"

"Let's just hope that she chooses wisely."

CHAPTER

TWO

"Dammit, Brayden, that's not funny! Give me back my laptop before I smack you with it!"

Knox Channing raised his head, cocking an eyebrow at his younger brother when he raced into the room, their hellcat sister on his heels. No one messed with Briar's computer. Not anyone with any brains, anyway. Something Brayden seemed to be sorely lacking this morning.

"All work and no play makes Briar a cranky cub," Brayden teased, throwing his head back and laughing when Briar crossed her arms over her chest and glared at him as she began tapping the floor with a foot.

"Not all of us can sit on our asses and do nothing all day," she snapped. "Maybe you should get a job and start contributing to the family income."

"Hey, we just moved here a couple of weeks ago," Brayden said, holding the laptop high above his head. "I'll get a job when I'm ready. What's wrong with having a little fun for now?"

"We've been here for a month," Noah said dryly, entering the kitchen and going straight for the coffee pot. He was dressed in a dark gray suit, with a burgundy tie and gold cuff links. "If you are going to spend all of your time at the titty bar, maybe you should put in an application there."

"Hasn't anyone ever told you that you don't work where you play?" Nolan asked, walking into the room, his jaw cracking from a wide yawn as he scratched at the thick patch of hair on his chest.

"Jesus Christ, Nolan, put on some fucking pants!" Briar screeched, right before she jumped up and snatched her laptop from Brayden's hands. Knox tensed when it slipped from her fingers, falling toward the floor, but Brayden caught it just before it landed and handed it to his sister. Which was good, because the next few days would have been hell for all of them if Briar would have had to wait on a replacement. She backed up everything to a server, and she had a desktop in her office, but the laptop was her baby. She took it with her almost everywhere she went.

Shaking his head, Knox took a long drink of his coffee, wishing he was already out with the horses. He would rather be scooping shit right now than listening to his family bicker this early in the morning.

"Get over it, little sister. We are all shifters here. Nudity isn't anything new to us."

"That doesn't mean we want to see your dick waving around in our faces all of the time," Noah groused, leaning back against the counter and taking a drink of his coffee.

"I second that," Briar snapped, but her deep amber eyes were dancing with laughter.

Knox glanced over to see his little sister, Miracle, standing in the doorway. She was dressed in a pale pink blouse with a flowing black skirt that stopped just above her knees. Her light blonde hair was pulled back away from her face, hanging in curls over her shoulders, and she wore a very subtle hint of makeup that accented her light blue eyes. Her gaze traveled around the kitchen, then came to rest on him. She sent him a small smile, but he could tell something was bothering her.

When the others started in on Nolan again, Knox decided he was done listening. It was their daily routine, one he didn't want to participate in today. Slamming his fist down on the table, he growled, "Enough!"

He saw Miracle's eyes widen in surprise, and then she instantly lowered her gaze to the floor, baring her neck, as did everyone else in the room. Since the death of their parents six months ago, he was in charge of their family. The alpha of what was left of the Channing bears. No one questioned him.

"Noah, go to work. You're going to be late, and you hate that. Brayden, it's time you found a job. I don't care if we need the money or not. You need something to keep you out of trouble. Briar, I need you to look over the financials. I'm looking into purchasing a new stallion in a couple of months, and it's going to be expensive. Nolan, go put some fucking pants on!" When they all looked at him in shock, unused to him giving orders the way he was, he snarled, "Go! Now!"

The room cleared out quickly, all except for Miracle,

who had snuck past them to get to some bagels that were sitting on the counter. Watching her slide one into the toaster, Knox took a sip of his coffee while he waited patiently for her to speak.

"That wasn't very nice," she finally said, after putting cream cheese on her bagel and bringing it over to the table.

He shrugged as she slid into the chair across from him and took a small bite of her breakfast. "They were annoying me."

Miracle giggled, like he hoped she would. "They act like that every day."

"They annoy me every day."

As Miracle giggled again, Knox reached over and placed his hand gently on her arm. "Talk to me, sis," he said quietly. "What's wrong?"

Moisture filled her eyes, and she lowered her gaze to stare at her plate. "I'm scared, Knox. I hate to admit that. I'm a grown woman. I shouldn't be this terrified just to leave the house on my own."

"You don't have to go anywhere," Knox told her, moving from his chair to kneel down beside her. "We talked about this, Miracle. There is absolutely no reason that you have to do anything you don't want to right now. You can stay home…"

"I can't," Miracle interrupted, shaking her head adamantly. "I refuse to hide behind you and the others, Knox. I won't."

Knox cupped her cheek, gently wiping away a tear with his thumb. "You are stronger than you think, Miracle. Even though I want you to stay home where I

13

can protect you, I know that isn't who you are. You may be scared, but you are going to face your fears, because you are a Channing now, and that is what we do."

Miracle nodded, lowering her head until their foreheads touched. "I will never forget what you did for me, Knox," she whispered. "What all of you did. What you gave up."

"Nothing in this world is more important than family," Knox said gruffly, rising and pulling her to her feet. "I regret nothing."

"Nor do any of the rest of us, little sis."

Knox turned to look at his brother, his eyes narrowing on the new button-down shirt and nice pair of jeans that Brayden wore. Arching an eyebrow, he asked, "Are you going job hunting this early?"

Brayden shrugged, his gaze going to Miracle. "I already have a job," he confessed. "I have for a week or so. I'm the new history teacher at the school."

Knox heard the breath hitch in Miracle's throat, and he looked down at her, worried that she was upset with Brayden for getting a job where she was about to start teaching herself. Brayden had taught geography where they lived before, but Knox just assumed he would go into a different field when they moved, like he did.

A wide smile spread across Miracle's face, and she crossed the room quickly to wrap her arms tightly around their brother. "Thank you," she whispered, as she leaned back and tugged on one of the short, light brown curls in his hair. "Thank you so much, Brayden. You don't know what this means to me."

Brayden cleared his throat, a faint blush stealing over

his cheeks. "Love you, sis," he said, returning her hug quickly, and then stepping back. "We better get going. Don't want to be late on our first day!"

Knox watched them leave, a slow smile turning up the corners of his mouth. Miracle was going to be fine. It would take a while, but once she realized that she was safe now, that no one was ever going to hurt her again, then she would come out of her shell.

"I'm glad Brayden is going to be there for her," Nolan said quietly, buckling his belt as he made his way down the hall toward him. "She's been through enough. She sure as hell doesn't need to be alone right now."

"She's not alone," Knox replied, walking back into the kitchen to clean up his mess. "She has us."

"You're damn right she does," Nolan snarled, "and no one is going to touch a hair on her head again. Not if they want to live."

Closing the dishwasher after placing his cup and Miracle's plate inside, Knox walked over to Nolan and bumped fists with him. "We protect what's ours, and Miracle is ours now."

Nolan nodded, a low growl filling his chest. "Damn straight."

Miracle may not be their sister by blood, but she was the sister of their hearts, and there wasn't anything anyone in the Channing family wouldn't do for her.

CHAPTER
THREE

She moaned softly when she felt something hit her cheek lightly, and reached up to swat it away. A sharp gasp escaped when she felt the pain and stiffness in her muscles. The soft touch came again, and she groaned, rubbing a hand over her face. Forcing her eyelids open, she stiffened when she met the bright green gaze of a black cat who was lying on her chest. The animal stared at her, cocking its head to the side as if wondering who she was.

"Hello," she whispered, resting a hand on the cat's back and petting it gently. A slow smile crept across her face when it meowed and shoved its head into her hand, demanding more attention.

"That's Cinder," a voice said from across the room. "She's my familiar."

Turning her head, she spotted a woman standing off to the other side of the room gazing out a window, with one hand resting on the clear glass. "Your what?" she croaked, as she lightly pushed the cat off her chest and struggled into a sitting position. Gritting her teeth, she fought back the wave of nausea that hit her. She couldn't remember ever feeling this horrible. She was a shifter, which meant she normally healed quickly, but this time it seemed to be taking longer than normal.

The woman turned with a smile and crossed the room to her. "My familiar. She showed up after I came into my powers, and is always with me now."

Her brow furrowed as she stared at the other woman, and then cleared when she realized who she was. "Aurora."

"Yes," Aurora said, sliding a chair over to the side of the bed and sitting down.

"You saved me," she whispered, tears filling her eyes.

Aurora shook her head, her dark green eyes warm as she replied, "No, Emery, you saved yourself. All I did was help a little."

"Emery. That's the new name you gave me." It was so hard to believe that she was starting a new life. One free of the hell she had gone through before... she hoped. What if they found her?

"Yes. It means powerful and brave, which you definitely are."

"I don't feel very brave right now," Emery confessed, clasping her hands tightly in her lap. "I can't stop thinking that I may have escaped them for now, but what if they manage to track me down?"

"Let's not dwell on the *what if* scenarios," Aurora said softly. "Let's concentrate on what *is*."

Emery took a deep breath and nodded, biting her lip. After a moment, she whispered, "I'm free. I'm not locked away where I can't see the moon at night, or have the sun shine on my face during the day. I'm not getting beaten and starved. Not being pressured to mate with someone who will only hurt me more. I'm going to start a new life."

"Yes, you are. That new life will only be what you make it, Emery Ericksen. So, make it a good one." Emery swore she saw hesitancy in the other woman's eyes before she went on, "There is only so much I can tell you, Emery. You have to make your own choices, your own decisions, to get to the path you will follow. Great things are destined for you, but there will come a time where you will have to make a choice. That will be fate's defining moment."

"When?" Emery whispered, giving in to the need to lie back down. She was too weak to stay upright, even though she hated to admit it.

"I can't tell you that," Aurora murmured, "but you will know."

"I'm getting tired," Emery said softly, her eyelids fluttering closed.

"Can you shift before you fall asleep?" Aurora asked, and Emery could hear the worry in her voice.

Fighting against the exhaustion that was taking over, Emery closed her eyes and tried to connect with her animal. There was no response. No sign at all that she was there. Letting out a frustrated moan, she shook her head. "No. I'm too weak."

"Okay," Aurora said, running a comforting hand down her arm. "Get some more rest. Everything will be better soon."

"Wait," Emery whispered, grasping Aurora's hand tightly in hers. "I have so many questions."

"I promise to answer them all," Aurora murmured, squeezing her hand gently, "but you need to sleep first. We will talk some more when you wake up."

Emery sighed, and letting go of Aurora's hand, she let herself fall back into a deep, healing sleep.

CHAPTER
FOUR

The next time Emery awoke, it was nightfall. It was dark, except for dying embers in the fireplace. The logs hissed and crackled when they shifted, and seemed to fall in on each other. She couldn't tear her gaze away from the small flames, her eyes misting over as she thought about how messed up her life was. She would now be running for the rest of her life after leaving her herd, and the alpha who wanted to claim her as his own, the way she did. She would never feel safe again, not that she had in a long time.

"How are you feeling?"

Emery stiffened when the soft voice drifted over to her. Tilting her head back slightly, she saw Aurora standing in the doorway, a look of concern on her face, along with something else. Determination. The woman was determined to protect her, no matter the cost, Emery realized. She couldn't remember the last time anyone had cared enough about her to want to keep her safe.

"I'm sorry. I didn't mean to startle you," Aurora

whispered, crossing the room to throw a couple more logs on the fire. "It gets chilly at night, and I wanted to make sure you were as warm as possible after everything you've been through."

Emery struggled into a sitting position, and then slowly let her gaze wander around the dark room, lit only by the fire, before responding, "Thank you. I appreciate it."

Aurora was quiet for a moment, before she said, "Do you want to try to shift now?"

"I would rather talk, if that's okay?" She was still exhausted, and just didn't have the energy to coax her animal to the surface. Not just yet.

Aurora nodded, sitting in the chair that was still beside the bed Emery lay in, before saying, "What would you like to know?"

Emery asked the question that had been plaguing her since she found out that someone was coming to rescue her from the nightmare she was in. "Why? Why would you put your life on the line to help me? You don't even know me."

A gentle smile crossed Aurora's lips, and Emery swore her eyes began to glow in the darkness. "Because no one deserves to live the way you were being forced to live, Emery. Without kindness and love. In pain, suffering from the hands of your own family. In constant fear of what the future holds."

"You've done this before," Emery said, watching the other woman closely. It wasn't a question. There was no way this was Aurora's first time saving someone's life. It was in her eyes, those captivating green eyes that seemed to glow even brighter than before. The passion in them was unmistakable. What she did, helping others who could not defend themselves, meant everything to her.

"I was once where you are now," Aurora admitted quietly. "Alone and afraid, with no one who cared enough to step forward and save me from the situation I was in. I refuse to sit back and watch it happen to others if I can do something about it."

"How many women have you saved?"

Aurora shrugged, glancing over at the fire as she murmured, "The number doesn't matter. The people do."

"You've saved men, too," Emery whispered in understanding.

Meeting her gaze, Aurora replied, "I help anyone who needs it, Emery. I do not discriminate."

"I didn't mean..."

"I know what you meant," Aurora said, holding up a hand to quiet her. "My sisters and I have helped many over the years, and will continue to do so for as long as we live."

"Sisters?"

Aurora's eyes lit with love as she replied, "My coven."

"Witches," Emery breathed in awe. Before Aurora, she had never met a witch before. She'd thought they were myths, legends made up by people long ago.

"Yes."

"How many of you are there?" Emery whispered, real hope beginning to fill her for the first time in a long time. From what she knew of the legends, witches were very powerful. Maybe, just maybe, she would be safe for a little while after all. At least until she could get back on her feet and save up enough money to move on.

"There are nine in my coven," Aurora told her. "I cannot give you much more information than that about my sisters. We prefer to keep to ourselves, and keep our identities secret, for obvious reasons."

Emery nodded, her mind racing with questions. She wanted to respect the other woman's privacy, but she couldn't help but ask, "Is that how you were able to speak to me in my mind at the waterfalls? I remember your voice in my head telling me to fight. I... I wouldn't have made it without you, Aurora."

Aurora seemed to hesitate, before murmuring, "As a witch, I have certain gifts that have been bestowed upon me. Telepathy is one of them."

When Aurora didn't elaborate, Emery knew it was time to change the subject. The witch had her secrets, and she should be allowed to keep them. Especially, if sharing them would somehow compromise her safety or that of her coven. Deciding there were a few other questions she wanted answered, she asked, "How did Meadow know how to contact you?"

Meadow. The terrified young woman who had reached out to her in the cells where she was being held, putting her own life in jeopardy. If Alpha Ramsey ever found out that it was his own daughter who freed Emery from hell, there was no telling what he would do to the poor girl.

Aurora's eyes lit with an emotion stronger than anything Emery had seen in her so far. Love. "I met sweet

23

Meadow years ago when she was just a child," Aurora said quietly. "No more than fourteen, but with a heart bigger than anything I had ever seen. She got my name from someone she met in school, someone I rescued and relocated to the town where Meadow lived. The moment I heard her voice, I knew she was destined for great things."

"You had a vision," Emery whispered, knowing it was true, even though Aurora didn't elaborate. How many other gifts did the witch have?

"Meadow was looking for help."

"I don't blame her. Her father is an ass. She has to live a hard life."

"She does," Aurora agreed, "but the help wasn't for her. It was for someone in a coyote pack two towns over that she met at a gathering she went to with her father. Alpha Ramsey was looking for allies in a war he wanted to start against a herd that moved in too close to his own. He wanted to kill the alpha of the herd, and then merge the two herds together, with himself as alpha over them all."

"I remember," Emery said softly. "I was just eighteen at the time. I remember, because it was just before I graduated from high school. He called my father and asked him to send some of our enforcers a couple of weeks before the war between the two herds actually started, but Dad told him no. It wasn't his fight, and he wanted nothing to do with it."

"Well, the coyotes didn't say no," Aurora told her. "In fact, they were the only reason Alpha Ramsey won."

"What did they get out of it?"

"Money, land, and three of the women from Ramsey's herd to do with as they pleased."

"Oh, my God," Emery gasped, her hand going to her throat. "He sold part of his own herd to coyotes?" It shouldn't have surprised her, though. The man was a bastard, through and through.

"Yes," Aurora whispered, "and they didn't survive long." Tears filled Emery's eyes as Aurora went on, "The women were given to them the night of the gathering. Handed over as if they were nothing more than cattle. Meadow watched what the coyotes did to them from where she sat by her father, unable to do anything about it. She told me that was when she decided she was done being helpless. When she met the female coyote shifter later that evening and became aware of what she was going through at the hands of her own pack, she took a stand."

"And she has been doing it ever since then," Emery guessed.

"Yes."

"She was terrified when she came to me, Aurora."

"She always is."

"Then it needs to stop."

Aurora sighed, running a hand through her thick hair. "I've tried to talk to her about it, Emery, but nothing I say changes her mind. She might be afraid, but she won't stop."

"Not afraid," Emery snapped. "Terrified!"

"Emery, there is nothing I can do for Meadow if she won't let me remove her from the situation."

25

"I want to help her," Emery whispered, "like she helped me."

"You can only help someone who wants to be helped," Aurora said quietly. "Meadow is not at a place where she is ready to focus on herself. Right now, she wants to save others."

"Like me," Emery whispered, one lone tear slipping free and sliding down her cheek.

"Yes, like you."

"But, what happens if her father figures out what she is doing? You know he will kill her."

Aurora looked down at her folded hands before raising her head again and meeting Emery's gaze. "Yes, he will, but it is her choice to make. Not ours."

"It's bullshit!"

There was a long moment of silence, and then Aurora murmured, "She will reach out to me someday, Emery. And, when she does, I will not hesitate to help her."

Emery swallowed hard, clenching the blanket that covered her tightly. "You've seen it?"

Aurora hesitated before nodding. "Yes. Not quite in the way you are thinking, and I can't tell you exactly what the future holds, but when she needs me, I will be there."

Gritting her teeth, Emery looked over at the fire in the hearth where flames were now flying high. The room was once again warm, and the heat sank into her bones, finally pushing away the chill from the night before. She knew Aurora was right, but she didn't want her to be. Thoughts of how she could get Meadow away from her father consumed her, but there was no way it was going to happen until the young woman was ready to leave. You could not save the unwilling.

Swallowing hard, Emery brought her gaze back to Aurora. "So, what's next?"

"For you?"

"Yes. Where do we go from here?"

Aurora smiled, reaching out to place a hand over one of Emery's. "For now, we focus on you regaining your strength. Then, I have a job lined up for you in town."

"I can't do anything to bring attention to myself," Emery protested, hating the way her body began to tremble in fear. She was stronger than this, dammit!

"You won't," Aurora promised. "You will be working as a waitress at the Lyon's Den serving drinks, and will be paid under the table."

"A bar?"

"Yes."

"And they are paying me cash? Under the table?"

"Yes."

"But, that's illegal."

Chuckling, Aurora squeezed her hand, and then sat back in her chair. "Yes, it is, but these are dire circumstances, and the owner understands."

"You told someone about me?"

"Not specifics. Garrith Lyons knows what I do," Aurora said softly. "He and his family have helped me in the past. Trust me, he will protect you while you are there, and he will never ask you questions about who you are, or where you are from. You will be safe."

Nodding slowly, Emery sighed, "I'm sorry. I want to trust you, Aurora, but it's so hard right now."

27

"I understand," Aurora replied gently, before rising to stand in front of her. "You've been through a lot. I don't expect you to trust anyone right away, not even me. Trust is earned."

"You've earned mine by coming for me when you didn't have to," Emery whispered. "It's just hard right now to fully put my trust in anyone."

"Especially, when you couldn't trust your own family."

Emery raised her eyes to meet Aurora's understanding gaze. "Yes."

"I get that, Emery. I've been there."

"Thank you." Moving the covers from her legs, Emery turned so they were dangling over the side of the twin bed she'd spent the last several hours in. "I'm ready to shift."

"Wonderful! Do you need some help?"

Taking a deep breath, Emery shook her head. "No, I've got this."

Aurora leaned in and gave her a quick hug, then stepped back. "Okay, I am going to go get some sleep now. I'm just up the stairs, and down the hall, second door on the left, if you need me."

When she started to leave the room, Emery spoke up, "Aurora, thank you again for all that you are doing for me. I don't know what I would have done without you."

Aurora glanced back, her eyes sparkling with warmth. "You would have survived, Emery, because that's who you are."

She left before Emery could respond, which was fine, because she had no idea what she would have said. Yes, she probably would have survived, but to what extent? As a hollow version of the person she was before, knowing that her family hadn't loved her enough to keep her with them. That, instead, they sold her to the highest bidder, uncaring that he was a beast from hell? That was no way to live. She wasn't sure she would have wanted to survive to experience that life.

Sighing, Emery slipped the nightgown that someone must have dressed her in after they reached the house, up and over her head. Next, she removed the white panties she wore. Once she was free and clear of all clothing, she curled up on the bed and called to her animal. It took longer than normal to initiate the shift, and it was a struggle to get through it, but finally, a small, caramel colored bunny with white throughout its fur lay where she had just been.

With another long sigh, she snuggled into the covers and closed her eyes, letting sleep overtake her. There would be enough time to worry about everything else later. Right now, she just needed to rest and get better. Then, she would consider her future.

A waitress, huh? This ought to be interesting.

CHAPTER
FIVE

"Come on, Knox," Brayden urged, a boyish grin on his face. "It will be fun."

"No."

"Just think about it. It's been a long time since you've been out."

He didn't have to think about it. Just the thought of going to a bar made him cringe. Loud music, dancing, not to mention the women who were always looking for someone to hook up with. He wanted no part of it. Hell, he could sit at home and have a beer in front of the television, which was exactly what he was doing. And, if he wanted to dip his dick into some willing female, he sure as hell wasn't going to do it in the town he lived in. Then they would expect some kind of commitment, and he had way too much on his plate right now. He didn't have time to play games.

"You're going, brother," Nolan said as he walked into the living room and tossed a beer in Brayden's direction.

"No, I'm not," Knox growled, taking a swig of the Budweiser he clutched almost too tightly in his hand.

"Please," Miracle said softly, as she entered the room.

Knox stiffened, slowly turning to look at his youngest sister, his eyebrows rising at the outfit she was wearing. A black dress hugged her slender body, stopping just above her knees. The neckline dipped down, showing more cleavage than Miracle had shown in months. Her makeup was darker than normal, and she stood at least three inches higher than normal in burgundy heels. "You're going to the bar?"

Miracle grinned nervously, "Yes, if you go."

Knox's scowl returned, and he motioned to his brothers. "Did they put you up to this?"

"No," Briar said as she breezed into the room and hooked her arm through Miracle's. "I did. I'm going, and I don't want to be the only girl in the group."

"You won't be for long," Knox groused, knowing he had just lost the battle. There was no way in hell he was letting both of his sisters go to the bar without his protection. Tipping his head back, he finished the beer, and then rose from his chair. "The minute Nolan walks through the door, he will be surrounded by women."

"Yes, but not by anyone I know."

She was right. They may have moved to Moonstone over a month ago, but Briar spent the majority of her time at home, like he did. They were definitely not the sociable ones of the family. The only people he'd actually met so far was the Lyons family when they first arrived. As a common courtesy, he went to their home to introduce himself and ask for permission to live in their

31

territory. Other than that, he stayed at the ranch, even going so far as to send Brayden or Nolan into town to get feed for his horses. Looked like that was going to change now.

"Where's Noah?" If Briar and Miracle were going to the bar, then *all* of his brothers would be there, too.

"Noah had to work late, so he's meeting us there."

Nodding, Knox glanced over at the clock on the wall. It was just after 8 p.m., which meant the Lyon's Den would probably be packed by now. While he may have never been there, all of his brothers had, and they liked to talk. Garrith Lyons' bar was one of the busiest places in town, besides his brother's strip club, and it was Friday night. A lot of people would be there wanting to let off some steam. A lot of men, who wanted to get in his sisters' pants. With a low growl at the thought, Knox strode from the room

"Hey, where are you going?" Brayden hollered.

"To get some damn jeans on," Knox snapped, knowing he didn't have a choice. He was about to change his soft, comfortable jogging pants, for a pair of jeans and a button-down shirt. It was time to fucking mingle, something he had never been good at.

Ten minutes later, Knox was ready to go. Looking in the mirror, he shrugged. He would pass. Placing his black Stetson on his head, Knox slid his wallet into the back pocket of his jeans and left his room. Time to paste a smile on his face and play nice for the evening.

Who was he kidding? He hardly ever smiled, and there was only one way he liked to play. Nice wasn't it.

CHAPTER
SIX

E mery stood by the bar, waiting for the bartender to fill her order. It was her second week at work, and she found that she actually enjoyed it. The owner and his wife were kind and respectful. They never asked questions about where she came from, how long she planned on sticking around, or what trouble she was in. And, for the most part, the people who came to the bar treated her with that same respect. There were a couple of men who tried to hit on her, but they backed off quickly when she shied away from them.

All except one. He was persistent, and even though he frightened her because she knew he was a wolf shifter and could eat her for dinner, he was really starting to piss her off, too. He'd shown up at the bar every night since she first started the job, and it was no secret that he was there for her.

"Everything okay, Emery?" the bartender asked, setting a margarita and two glasses of tap beer on the tray in front of her.

Emery looked up into his kind eyes, biting her lip as she let her gaze wander over to the corner where the wolf, Cyrus, was sitting. He'd deliberately sat in her section, which he did every night, and he was watching her closely. Clenching her teeth, Emery turned back to the bar, picking up the tray. "Yes, thank you, Cale. I'm fine."

Leaning closer, Cale said in a low voice, "If he is bothering you, all you have to do is say something, Emery. Garrith will kick his ass out, and make sure he knows to stay away from you."

A part of her knew that was true, but she couldn't bring herself to ask for help. If she was going to live on her own, she was going to have to learn how to fend for herself. Straightening her shoulders, Emery let her lips curl up into a small, fake smile. "I'm fine," she lied smoothly, gripping the tray tightly, "but, thank you, Cale."

Ignoring the fact that the stench of her lie filled the air, Emery winked at Cale and left to take the drinks to a table on the other side of the room. It was as far away from Cyrus as she could get, but still be in her section. She wondered how much longer it would be before the wolf made his move. She could feel him stalking her, and she was getting really fucking tired of being his prey.

Suddenly, the most tantalizing scent hit her, and Emery froze, her nose twitching slightly. She was glad the tray she held was now empty, or she might have embarrassed herself by dropping all of the drinks on the floor. Clutching the tray to her chest, she thanked the group of people in front of her, and slowly backed away, slipping into a small alcove toward the back of the bar.

What was that smell?

Breathing in deeply, Emery gasped when the scent flooded her nostrils, easing inside her, and sinking deep into her bones. Oh... my... God. It was like nothing she'd ever experienced before. She bit her lip as her nipples tightened into hard beads, and a bolt of lust shot like lightening straight through her body and down into her core, almost making her come right there. "No," she whispered softly in shock. "No, this is not fucking happening. Not now!"

Trying to get control of her hormones, Emery sucked in another deep breath, and then wanted to scream at her own stupidity when that mouth-watering scent filled her once again. She knew what it meant. She knew people in her old herd who had gone through something similar, and they would all sit around talking about it afterward. Emery had prayed it would happen to her someday, wanting nothing more than to feel what it was like, but not now. Not when she was on the run and didn't have a chance in hell of doing anything about it.

Her eyes misting with unshed tears at the unfairness of it all, Emery slowly took a step forward and looked around the room, trying to track where the smell was coming from. She had to see him. Her mate. The other half of her soul. Even if she couldn't claim him as her own right now, she needed to see him.

Emery's gaze landed on a table not far from her. One of *her* tables. There were three males and two females

35

pulling out chairs, and as she watched, a fourth male joined them.

Her eyes roamed over the men, stopping on one who was holding a chair out for the blonde. He was tall, so tall that he dwarfed the woman beside him. There was a seriousness about him, and also a protectiveness. He had thick, dark hair that she wanted to slide her fingers into, and dark brown eyes you could drown in. Her fingers itched to caress the hardness of his jawline, and his lips... she wondered what it would be like to trace them with her tongue.

Emery let her gaze travel over his wide shoulders, and down to his thick chest, a low growl slipping past her lips when they stopped on where his hands rested on the woman's shoulders. Who was she? And, why the hell was her mate touching her?

Suddenly, the reason why she should turn around and run wasn't important anymore. All that mattered was those large hands on the delicate woman sitting before him.

Emery took a step toward them, and then another, intent on the man in front of her, when suddenly, he raised his head and inhaled, his nostrils flaring. His hands must have tightened on the woman, because she raised her head to look at him, looking as if she were asking him a question.

Satisfaction filled Emery when he didn't bother to answer her, and slowly removed his hands, placing them on his hips as he gazed around the room. When those deep, brown eyes settled on her, Emery's heart began to pound, and the tip of her tongue snuck out to wet her dry lips. His eyes seemed to center on her mouth, and he took a step in her direction.

Emery was unaware of what was going on around her. She could not tear her gaze away from the man.

Her mate.

"Emery." She heard the voice, but couldn't focus on it. She needed to be closer to *him*. "Emery, is everything all right?" Emery jumped when she felt the hand on her arm, the light touch snapping her out of the trance she'd been in. Swallowing hard, she turned to look at Tatum Lyons, Garrith's wife. Her light brown eyes were filled with concern, and the hold on her arm tightened. "Emery?"

Before she could ask again, Emery forced herself to smile, gently pulling from her grasp. "Everything is fine," she lied, glancing back over to where the man still stood, his eyes never leaving her. "I'm just getting a little tired."

Tatum took the tray from Emery, and slipped an arm around her waist, guiding her over to a table even closer to the object of her obsession. "Take all the time you need, sweetheart. I can take the order for the new table while you rest."

"No!" Emery shook her head, refusing to sit at the table. "They are in my section. I will handle it." For some reason, it was very important that she be the one to take care of her mate. No one else. Especially, not another female, even if she did already have a mate of her own.

Tatum's brow furrowed in confusion, and she pointed to the chair. "Emery, sit your ass down, now."

Emery's eyes widened at the tone in her voice, but she still refused to sit. "No, it's my table. I will handle it."

Pulling out a chair, Tatum plopped in the seat, once again motioning to the other one. "I didn't say you couldn't handle it, Emery, but they can wait a few minutes. You need to take a break, and I am going to sit here with you while you do."

Emery sighed, knowing arguing with the woman was useless. She'd seen Tatum Lyons' in action before, and she just wasn't up to sparring with her right now. Collapsing in the chair opposite her, Emery said hoarsely, "I'm sorry, Tatum. I don't know what came over me."

Liar. She knew exactly what had come over her, but she wanted to keep her secret a while longer. It wasn't like she was going to act on it, anyway. Was she?

Tatum was saying something, but Emery wasn't aware of what it was. Her eyes slid back over to the table where her mate was again, and she couldn't seem to look away. He was staring at her, his hands clenched tightly into fists at his sides, the tips of his fangs barely peeking out from his top lip.

His fangs. Damn. What would it feel like to have him sink them deep into her skin? A soft moan left her lips as desire began to pool in her belly.

"Emery, do you need to go home?"

Emery shook her head, licking her lips, her gaze never leaving her mate's mouth.

"Emery!"

Blinking, Emery shook her head, aware that she was making an utter fool of herself, but unable to stop. "I'm sorry. No, I don't need to leave."

Yes, she did. She needed to run as far and as fast as

she could away from Moonstone, and the man who just took another step in her direction.

As she watched, the woman with the long, light blonde hair stood and placed a hand on his arm. When she looked up at him with her big blue eyes, leaning into him to speak softly, it was all Emery could do to not to jump across the distance that separated them and tear her throat out.

Who was she? And why did it look so natural for her to touch him like that? Maybe he hadn't waited for his fated mate like she had. Maybe he settled for love instead? Maybe... maybe the woman who was now looking over toward them was his wife.

Dark pain engulfed her at the thought, and Emery rose quickly, dropping her tray on the table. Had he forsaken her, his true mate, for love? Was that it?

"Actually, I think I do need that break," Emery ground out, looking down into Tatum's startled expression. "I'll be back in ten minutes, if that's okay?"

"Of course," Tatum said, before reaching out to grab her by the wrist. "Emery, I'm here if you need me. I can help you. My family, my husband's family, we can all help you."

Emery's bottom lip began to tremble, and she nodded, pulling away from the other woman and slowly stepping back. "Thank you, but everything is fine."

That must be her new motto. Everything is fine. Hell, she'd sure said it enough tonight. Without another word, she turned and almost ran to the other side of the bar, ignoring the surprised gazes of some of the Lyon's Den's patrons. Finding sanctuary in the bathroom, she crossed to the sink and splashed water on her pale face, and then stared at herself in the mirror. Wide eyes full of both desire and fear stared back.

What was she going to do now? What the hell was she going to do?

SEVEN

"Knox, I don't know what's going on, but you need to sit your ass down, man."

Turning to his brother, Knox bared his teeth and snarled, "Don't tell me what the fuck to do."

"Knox, please," Miracle whispered, tugging on his arm, "sit down. People are beginning to stare."

Only the thought of what it did to his sister to be put on display like that made Knox finally relent and fall into the chair next to her, but his gaze never left the place where his beautiful mate had disappeared to. "What's down that hall?" he demanded roughly, his voice garbled through the large, thick fangs he was having trouble hiding.

"Just the bathrooms," Brayden told him, and Knox could hear the shock in his voice.

"Nothing else? No exit?"

"No," Brayden said hesitantly, "I don't think so."

Knox turned to look at him, baring his teeth once again, "No, or you don't think so? What's the answer?"

Because if there was a way for his gorgeous, curvy-as-hell mate to get away from him down that hall, he sure as shit wasn't going to sit there patiently waiting for her to come back.

"No," Nolan cut in, saving his little brother from Knox's anger. "There are only two ways out of the Lyon's Den. The front door, and the exit into the back alley down that hall over there."

Knox nodded, glancing over to where Nolan indicated. "Good. That's good."

"Who is she to you?" a voice asked softly from beside them, and Knox had to reign in his temper before looking over at the woman.

"That's none of your business," he growled lowly, his gaze connecting with the female lioness'.

"Actually, it is my mate's business, and I suggest you start talking, bear."

Knox stiffened when Garrith Lyons' scent hit him, and he realized that he'd just royally screwed up. Consumed with thoughts of his own mate, he had inadvertently offended the son of Moonstone's alpha.

"I apologize," he said stiffly, tilting his head slightly to the side. His gaze going back to the hallway where his mate had disappeared, he said, "I meant no disrespect."

"I will ask you one more time, bear," Garrith growled. "Who is she to you?"

"Mine," Knox told him, willing his fangs to recede so that he could talk normally. "She's mine."

"Oh, no," Tatum whispered, her hand going up to cover her mouth. "This is bad, Garrith. This is really bad."

A slow smile crossed Garrith's face as he met Knox's confused gaze. "Or, it could be very good."

"Garrith..."

"Tatum, have you ever seen a grizzly bear in action? Those things are huge, and they protect what's theirs."

"She's not a piece of freaking meat, Garrith Lyons! She's a human being."

"Well, technically she's not."

"Oh, shut up, cat!" Tutum snapped, slapping her husband on the arm.

"Well, she's not."

"And she's not deaf, either!"

Knox's gaze swung from the couple to the woman who now stood just a couple of feet from him. She was so close that he could reach out and touch her, and she was simply amazing. All of the blood in his body immediately headed south, his cock stiffening at the fire in her eyes. Thick, caramel colored hair, with what looked to be white highlights, flowed over her shoulders, covering the swell of her full breasts, and landing at her waist. Her eyes were a deep, dark blue, but were sparkling brightly with emotion now. Her lips so full, and pouty, and her skin, holy hell. He wanted to touch it to see if it was as soft as it looked.

"Emery, I'm sorry," Garrith said quietly, reaching out for her.

Knox growled when Emery flinched, jumping quickly away from the man, raising an arm as if to block a hit coming her way, but then seemed to catch herself. Crossing her arms under her full breasts, pushing them up even more than they already were, she said, "What I

43

am, or am not, is no one else's business unless I choose to tell them. I would appreciate it if you would please not discuss me when I'm not in the room."

"You're right," Miracle interjected, slowly lowering herself down in the seat next to him. "It was rude of us. I apologize."

Emery's gaze settled on his sister, and she seemed to be fighting a battle inside herself, before she finally said, "You have nothing to apologize for. What can I get all of you to drink?"

At the swift change of subject, it took Knox a minute to catch up, as his sisters quickly placed their orders, and then his brothers. When it came time for him, Emery bit her lip, and then asked, "And, for you?"

Fuck. Those full, pouty lips. That's what he wanted. What would she say if he ordered them?

There was soft laughter, and then Miracle said, "My brother always drinks Budweiser. Or sometimes whiskey if he's had a bad day, but it's normally beer."

"Your brother?"

Knox watched Emery's small nose twitch, and knew she was inhaling their scents. He also knew she would find that he and his sister smelled absolutely nothing alike. He was a bear, while Miracle was something altogether different. "Yes," he said gruffly, "Miracle is my sister. They are all my brothers and sisters."

When his mate's cheeks flooded a dark red, and she turned away quickly to head toward the bar, he almost followed her. Only Noah's quiet voice stopped him. "She obviously thought you and Miracle were together, Knox.

No wonder she ran. If I met my mate, and she had some other man draped all over her, all bets would be off."

"But, I wasn't draped all over Knox," Miracle protested.

"No, sis, you weren't," Briar cut in, "but you have to see it from her point of view. She has no idea who any of us are. And, well, you were touching Knox, and he had his hands on you."

"Fuck," Knox growled, sliding his chair back to go find his mate.

"It's too late," Tatum said, looping her arm through her husband's. "I think we all overwhelmed her. She just slipped out the back door after ordering your drinks."

"Dammit!" Knox snarled, slamming his fist into the table. Ignoring the glances other people in the bar were sending his way, he rose and quickly crossed the room to where his brother had said the back exit was. He was not going to let her run from him. Not until he had a taste of those lips first, at least. Then, and only then, would he give her some time to think. But, not much time. She was his, and he wasn't giving her up for anything.

EIGHT

E mery shoved a hand through her long, thick hair, swearing softly as she squeezed her eyes shut tightly. Leaning back against the brick wall in the alley behind the Lyon's Den, she took a deep breath, trying to clear her mind and body of the man's tantalizing scent. She needed to think clearly if she was going to get through the rest of the night. As much as she wanted to say screw it, jump into the old pickup truck Aurora was letting her borrow and run back to the farmhouse she currently lived in with the witch, she knew it wasn't an option. The bottom line was, she needed money, and she needed it now. Her brother and Alpha Ramsey would be looking for her, and she needed to leave town as soon as she had enough saved up to last until she could find another place to hide. That's what her life was going to be like from now on. Always running.

She stiffened when the door next to her was flung open, slamming hard against the wall on the opposite side of where she stood, but didn't bother to open her eyes when his scent filled the area around her. Dammit, she should have just kept going when she walked out of the bar a few minutes ago.

"You're still here," he said gruffly.

Emery heard the door shut, and sensed that he was moving, but refused to open her eyes to look at him. "Where else would I be?"

"Running from me," he growled, and Emery stiffened when she realized he was standing right in front of her. "From this. From us."

His low, gravelly voice sent a tremor of arousal through her, and Emery squeezed her thighs together tightly as she fought against the desire rising in her. Her skin felt hot, her breasts heavy, and there was a throbbing in her clit that just wouldn't stop. Swallowing hard, she snuck a peek at him from below slightly raised eyelids. "There is no us." There couldn't be. She wouldn't be around long enough for anything to happen.

"Fate doesn't seem to agree with you." When she didn't respond, he stepped closer to her, leaning in and whispering, "You're mine, little..." he paused, breathing in deeply, and then frowned as he finished, "bunny?"

She almost laughed at the incredulous look on his face. She'd known from the start that he wasn't like her. He was definitely the predator, while she was the prey. Why did she always have to be the prey? Why couldn't she be something cooler than a damn rabbit, like a tiger, or a freaking dragon. She could seriously kick ass if she was a dragon.

"I think fate might have really messed up this time," Emery whispered, tilting her head back to meet a gaze that was beginning to darken with pure lust. "Bears eat bunnies... and not in a good way."

A deep growl rumbled in his chest, and his eyes lit with fire as he promised, "Trust me, sweet bunny, I'm going to eat you in a *very* good way."

Emery's hands went to his chest, his very hard, thick chest, as a low moan left her throat at the thought of him kneeling before her and following through on that promise. The sane, reasonable part of her wanted to push him away, but there was a bigger part of her that wanted to give in and pull him closer, and she was afraid that horny bitch was going to win. "I don't even know your name."

Lowering his head, he slowly rubbed his face up the side of her neck, letting out a low groan. "Knox," he rasped, moving his face to the other side of her neck and marking her there. Because, that's what he was doing. Marking her as his, spreading his scent all over her, so that all other shifters would know she was taken. She let him, because even though she had no intention of staying in Moonstone, fate had chosen, which meant she would always be his, no matter what. "Knox Channing."

A small moan slipped free when he followed the curve of her neck with his tongue, stopping at the hollow of her throat and sucking gently. "This won't work."

Knox chuffed lightly, sending shivers down her spine when his warm breath hit her skin, wet from his tongue. "We will figure out a way to make it work."

Tears filled Emery's eyes, and she shoved lightly at his chest. "It's hopeless, Knox."

"Nothing is hopeless, sweet bunny," he rasped, right before his hot mouth covered hers.

Emery gasped in shock, and his tongue slipped past her lips, tangling with her own. She couldn't stop herself from responding. The sensations running through her were just too much. His taste was wild, intoxicating, and she wanted more.

Sliding her hands up and over his shoulders, she tugged him closer. Her body trembled as he grasped her hips tightly, pulling her flush against him, and she shuddered when she felt the thick length of his cock pressing into her. Tearing her mouth from his, she dug her nails into his back as she moaned, "Knox, wait. You have to wait."

Knox groaned, raising his heated gaze to meet her own. She saw the struggle in him, the same one she fought herself, before he asked gruffly, "Why are you running from this, Emery?" When she didn't respond right away, he stepped back, removing his Stetson and raking a hand through his short hair. "I'm sorry. I don't mean to push you."

"It's not that," she whispered, reaching a hand out to touch him, before slowly letting it fall to her side instead.

His dark eyes narrowing, Knox replaced his Stetson, and then braced his legs slightly apart, his hands on his hips. Her eyes were immediately drawn down to the thick bulge between his legs, and she clenched her hands tightly into fists, resisting the urge to close the distance between them and finish what they started just moments before. "Then what is it?"

"It's not you," she whispered.

49

"Are you seriously going to give me the 'It's not you, it's me' speech?" Knox growled in anger. "We haven't even gone out on a date, yet, Emery. You know nothing about me. How can you reject me already?"

"Because, I have no other choice," Emery whispered, shaking her head as a tear slipped free, slowly sliding down her cheek. "Goodbye, Knox."

Not waiting for a response, she walked away from him without a backward glance.

NINE

E mery sat curled up on the small twin bed in front of the fire, wrapped in a warm comforter, as she tried to make sense of everything that was happening to her. Was this fate's idea of some kind of cruel joke? Send her the other half of her soul, just to rip him away again? Why? What had she ever done to deserve the life she'd been born into?

"Maybe she isn't punishing you, Emery," Aurora said quietly from the doorway. "Maybe this is her way of paying you back for what you've had to endure so far."

Emery glanced over at her, grasping the comforter tightly. "So, you read minds, too?"

Aurora shrugged, walking into the room to stoke the fire. "You are broadcasting loudly. It's hard not to hear your thoughts."

"Do you ever think of your mind reading trick, and whatever else you can do, as more of a curse than a gift?" Emery asked, slipping her arms around her legs, and pulling them up to rest her chin on her knees.

"Sometimes," Aurora admitted softly, turning to look at her. "But, then I just remind myself of how many people I've been able to help, how many lives I've been able to save, using my gifts. The good definitely outweighs the bad."

Emery nodded, staring across the room into the flames. "I'm sure you already know this," she said softly, "but, I met my mate tonight."

Aurora came over to sit next to her, murmuring, "A mate is a blessing."

"Normally, I would agree," Emery whispered, laying her cheek on her knees to look over at Aurora. "This time, I'm not so sure."

The witch smiled, reaching over to slip a piece of wayward hair behind Emery's ear. "A mate is always a blessing, Emery. I know life is hard for you right now. You have no idea what the future holds. But, don't be afraid to find out."

"I can't put Knox and his family in that position, Aurora. What if one of them gets hurt? It would be my fault."

"No," Aurora replied, shaking her head. "You can't think of it that way, Emery. You have no control over what is going to happen. None of us do. It is what it is."

"I can't put my happiness first," Emery whispered.

"Maybe it's about time you did."

Raising her head, Emery glanced back into the flames. "No, survival must come first. Then, hopefully, happiness once I know I'm safe."

"Why can't you have both?"

Emery frowned, glancing back over at her new friend. "I don't understand."

"Emery, do you even know what true happiness is?"

"I..." Emery paused, thinking back on her life. "Yes," she finally whispered, swallowing hard. "I was happy when my father was still alive."

"Why? What made that part of your life so much different than the rest of it?" When Emery looked at her, one eyebrow raised, Aurora laughed softly. "I mean besides the obvious reasons. What did you have then, that you haven't had since?"

Emery hesitated, taking a moment to consider the question, before she realized what the answer was. "Love. My dad loved me, unconditionally. I haven't felt that since. I didn't realize until after his death, that my mother and brothers never really cared about me like he did."

"So, wouldn't you like to have that again?" Aurora asked quietly.

"Yes," Emery admitted, "I would. But, just because we are mates, doesn't mean that Knox loves me. We just met."

"Maybe not now, but he will. Someday. He's the other half of your soul, Emery. Fate gave him to you for a reason. If I were ever to be blessed with that kind of gift, I would like to think that I would stop at nothing to keep it."

"If my brother or Alpha Ramsey finds me, they will kill him."

"They would try," Aurora agreed.

"I couldn't live with myself if something happened to Knox or his family because of me."

"You only have one mate in the world, Emery. Don't give him up because of your fears. Fight for what you want."

"What if I'm not strong enough?" Emery whispered.

"You are."

"What if he isn't?"

Aurora laughed, rising from the bed. "Have you ever met a bear shifter, Emery?"

"No."

The witch's eyes lit with mischief as she leaned in and said, "Let me just tell you this, girl. Knox isn't the one you need to be worried about right now. Shifters in general are a possessive bunch, which you know. But, bears? They are altogether something different. Once that grizzly stakes his claim on you, all bets are off. And if anyone makes the mistake of getting in the way, trust me, they will regret it." Right before she left the room, Aurora looked back and smiled, "By the way, Knox Channing and his family bought the ranch just a mile south of here. I'm sure they wouldn't mind some company tomorrow, if you decide to stick around a little longer."

Emery watched her go, before sliding down on the bed and closing her eyes. Inhaling deeply, she let what was left of Knox's scent on her body envelop her. Maybe Aurora was right. Maybe she could stay, at least for a few more weeks. And maybe she would slip over to the Channing ranch tomorrow, just to catch a glimpse of her big bear. Maybe. What could it hurt?

TEN

K nox cursed loudly when he slammed the hammer down on his thumb on accident. It wouldn't have happened if he'd been paying attention to what he was doing, instead of thinking about wide, dark blue eyes, and sexy, pouty lips he wanted wrapped around his dick. He couldn't get his curvy bunny off his mind, and it was driving him fucking crazy.

"I'm sorry if I messed everything up for you last night, Knox."

Taking a deep breath, Knox turned to look at his youngest sister. Miracle stood at the entrance of the barn, her arms wrapped tightly around her waist as she stared dejectedly at the floor in front of her. When the smell of her tears hit him, he sat down the hammer and closed the distance between them. Pulling her close, he kissed her softly on the top of her head. "It isn't your fault, sprite."

"It is," Miracle insisted. "She thought we were together, and it upset her."

"Emery knows you are my sister, Miracle."

"But, does she believe it?" Miracle persisted. "I mean, you and I know that I am, but you have to admit, Knox, it would be awful hard for another shifter to believe I'm a Channing. Technically, I'm not."

"You are in all ways that count."

"I don't look like any of you, act like you, talk like you. I don't even smell like you, Knox."

"I don't give a shit," he snarled. "None of that matters. You are our sister, Miracle Channing, and that is all anyone else needs to know."

"But..."

"Stop, right now." Leaning back, Knox took her hand and walked over to a bale of hay. Lowering himself on top of it, he tugged her down next to him. "Miracle, Emery's leaving last night had absolutely nothing to do with you."

"Are you sure?"

Was he sure? Hell yeah, he was. It was all him. The moment he touched her, she'd gone up in flames, and it scared the shit out of her. "There's something more going on with Emery than any of us saw last night. From what Garrith said, it sounds like she's in trouble."

"Then, we need to help her."

That was his little sister, so full of kindness and love for everyone. She would do anything and everything she could for someone in trouble, it didn't matter who they were. Unfortunately, her giving spirit had gotten her in hot water more than once in the past. "We will," he promised. "I just have to figure out what's going on."

Miracle nodded, leaning into him. Resting her head

on his shoulder, she whispered, "I hope she's okay, Knox."

Knox was getting ready to respond, when the scent of his mate wafted around them. Frowning, he glanced around the area, looking for the object of his obsession. She was nowhere to be found. Sighing, thinking that he must be losing it, he closed his eyes and muttered, "She will be, sis. I'll make sure of it."

Emery's nose twitched as she watched the two in front of her. Knox sat close to Miracle, his arm around her shoulders, her head on his chest. Her long, light blonde hair flowed over his chest, her hand resting lightly on his thigh. She should have been pissed that he was that close to a woman who was clearly not related to him by blood, but she wasn't. The woman's eyes were full of tears, and she was surrounded in sadness. There was no attraction between the two, at all. There was love, but it was obviously the love of a sibling, and nothing more.

"What can we do for her, Knox?"

"I promise you, Miracle, Emery will be fine. You have nothing to worry about. I take care of my family. You, of all people, should know that."

They were talking about her? This sweet woman was crying for her?

Emery moved a little closer, worry filling her at the fear that radiated from Miracle.

"I know, Knox. I wouldn't be here today, if it wasn't

for you." She paused, and then whispered, "What if someone is hurting her? Like they were me?"

Emery moved closer still, wanting to somehow stop the tears that were now flowing from Miracle's eyes. She froze when she saw Knox move out the corner of her eye, knowing she'd messed up and given away her presence. Slowly, turning her head, she looked up at him.

"If anyone hurts what is mine, they will answer to me." The voice was hard, unyielding, possessive. His eyes were now on her, and she felt her heart flutter in her chest. Not in fear, though. In anticipation.

"Like the Howard brothers," Miracle whispered. It wasn't a question, and the pain and loss in her voice was almost enough to make Emery shift and go to the woman.

"Exactly like the Howard brothers."

Suddenly, Miracle seemed aware that they weren't alone. Raising her head, she wiped the tears from her eyes and looked in Emery's direction. "Oh! How beautiful!"

"Yes," Knox agreed, not moving from where he was, "she's very beautiful."

Emery hopped closer, waiting for Miracle to recognize her. It didn't take long. "Emery! You're a bunny!"

Why did everyone sound so damn surprised that she was a freaking rabbit? Did they not have rabbits in this town?

Knox chuckled, slowly leaning down and slipping his large hands underneath her. Lifting her onto his lap, he ran a hand gently over the soft, thick fur on her back.

"Don't be upset, sweetheart. You're the first rabbit shifter we've seen. I didn't even know they existed until last night."

Emery huffed, as much as she could in bunny form, and then hopped from his lap to Miracle's. The girl was still upset, and she couldn't stand to see the tears in her eyes. Butting her head up against Miracle's hand, she let out a small squeak. Miracle giggled, scratching the top of her head lightly. "Your fur is so soft," she whispered. "And, you are so small."

"I think she might be trying to tell you something, Miracle."

Miracle whispered, "You know Knox is my brother, right?" When Emery cocked her head to the side, as if questioning the accuracy of that statement, Miracle's lips turned up into a small smile. "The Channing's adopted me into their family after my own was killed. I don't know what I would have done without them. There's no way I would have survived."

Emery let out another small squeak, burrowing closer to the woman who was so full of pain and suffering. She had such a sweet, gentle soul, but seemed almost as if she were lost, somehow.

"Miracle, why don't you run inside and get Emery something to wear? Maybe she would like to have lunch with us?"

"Oh, yes! I'll be right back!"

All of a sudden, Emery found herself back on Knox's lap, and Miracle was off the hay bale and out the barn door in an instant. Which meant she was alone, with her mate.

"It's okay," Knox said softly, gently stroking her fur. "You don't have to shift if you don't want to, Emery. I was just trying to distract my little sister. She's been through so much, and I don't want her to relive it all right now."

Emery's heart warmed at the love in Knox's voice for his sister. From what she'd seen so far, he was a good man. She wanted to know more. Closing her eyes, she leaned into him, and waited to see if he would speak. She didn't have to wait long.

"Why don't I tell you a little about myself while we wait for her to return? Afterwards, you can decide if you would like to come eat with us, or if you would like to go home?"

Emery snuggled closer into him, hoping it would let him know that she was open to his plan.

"Good," Knox said softly, "that's good." He seemed to be collecting his thoughts, and then he went on, "Well, you know my name is Knox. Knox Channing. I am technically the oldest of six siblings. I say technically, because I'm a triplet. There's me, Noah, and Nolan, but I was born first. Then Brayden and Briar are twins. And, the youngest is Miracle. She's not ours by blood, but we claimed her as ours after the death of her own family." Emery heard the sadness creep into his voice and knew that he must have been close to Miracle's family, when they were alive. She wondered if they grew up together.

"We are all that are left of the Channings now. Our parents were taken from us a few months ago, and we recently moved to Moonstone to start a new life." She sensed the pain in him, but he seemed to ignore it as he said, "In my past life, I was in law enforcement, but now, I raise horses. I enjoy it." Somehow, Emery knew there was a lot more to the story than Knox was telling her. She had so many questions, but none she could ask unless she shifted. She didn't know if she was ready for that just yet.

"Do you miss being a cop?" Miracle asked, from where she now stood tentatively just inside the barn.

The hand on her back stilled, and she looked up to see Knox watching his sister closely. "Miracle, I do not regret any of the decisions I've made in the past. Not one."

"That doesn't answer my question," Miracle persisted. "Do you miss it?" She seemed so vulnerable, as if his response meant everything to her.

Emery felt Knox stiffen beneath her, and somehow knew that if he told Miracle the truth, it would hurt the girl more than help. Before she could think twice, Emery hopped from Knox's arms, and began to shift.

ELEVEN

Knox stood quickly when his mate jumped from his lap and initiated her shift. She was a thing of beauty, all legs, and hips, and curves that didn't stop. Her hair fell to just above her heart-shaped ass, and he was instantly hard at the thought of closing the distance between them and slipping into her from behind. That was definitely something he was going to do in the future.

"Thank you for bringing me something to wear." Her voice broke through his thoughts. The husky tone sliding over him, making him even harder, if that was possible.

"Of course!"

Even the fact that his sister was near wasn't enough to deflate his rock-hard cock. It seemed to have a mind of its own. Reaching down, he adjusted himself, wincing at the slight pain of being constricted in his Wranglers. Fuck, he needed to get control of himself before he came in his jeans like a damn teenager.

"We will be inside soon," Emery said, slipping a tee-shirt over her head and pulling her hair out from underneath the back of it. It was huge on her, stopping just below her thighs, and satisfaction filled Knox when he realized it was one of his own.

He was distantly aware of his sister leaving, but he couldn't seem to tear his gaze away from the beauty in front of him. As he watched, she slid one foot into a pair of black yoga pants, and then the other, sliding them up over that delectable ass, covering it up and hiding it from him. That, he didn't like.

Quickly closing the gap between them, Knox grasped her hips in his hands and pulled her back against him. When she moved as if to step away, he tightened his grip. "Please, just give me this."

Emery paused, and then slowly leaned back against him. "Just for a moment," she whispered. "Then, we need to go inside."

Nodding, even though she couldn't see him, he lowered his head toward her neck, closed his eyes, and breathed in deeply. His mate.

"Why are you fighting this?" he asked, knowing his tone was gruff, but unable to help it. He hadn't planned on his life changing the way it did the night before, but he wasn't going to ignore it. He wanted this. He wanted her.

Emery didn't respond right away. He thought that she wasn't going to, but then she whispered, "Because, it isn't safe."

Stiffening at the comment, Knox growled, "Why?"

Emery leaned her head back against his shoulder and sighed. "Can we talk about it later, Knox? Please?"

Knowing he couldn't make her tell him anything, Knox placed a gentle kiss on her cheek. "Later." When she tilted her head back to look up at him, he said gruffly, "Thank you for what you did earlier. With Miracle."

"I couldn't stand to see her in pain."

"None of us can," Knox replied, sliding his arms around her waist and holding her close.

"Those men, the Howard brothers, they hurt her?"

"In more ways than one."

"And, you killed them?"

"Yes." It was said in a cold, hard voice, and without remorse. "I meant what I said earlier, Emery. I take care of what's mine. It is my duty to protect my family. One I don't take lightly." When her eyes widened, but she didn't respond, he went on, "And, thank you for what you did for me."

"For you?"

Knox smiled, leaning down to place a gentle kiss on her lips. "For shifting when you did."

Emery didn't try to deny it. A small smile crossed her lips, and she whispered, "You're welcome."

"Hungry?"

"Not really."

Knox grinned, "Me neither, but if we stay out here alone much longer, I can't promise you that I will be able to continue to behave." Rubbing his still hard cock against her to prove his point, he growled, "Let's go see what's for lunch."

"As long as it isn't rabbit," she said under her breath.

"I'm sure we have some of that in the freezer if you'd like?"

When she looked up at him in horror, Knox threw his head back and laughed. The elbow to the gut came out of nowhere, and before he knew it, he was bending over trying to catch his breath. She'd hit him! His fucking mate had slammed her elbow into him. Hard. "You remember that the next time you think about eating Thumper!"

"It was a joke, woman!" But she was already gone, flouncing out of the barn and up to the house, not waiting to see if he followed.

When he glanced over to see Brayden watching from where he'd entered the barn through a side door, he pointed at him and growled, "Not a word, brother. Not a fucking word!"

His eyes dancing with mischief, Brayden grinned. "This is going to be fun."

"What is?" Knox snarled, even though he wasn't really pissed.

"Watching you fall," Brayden said, before walking past him, following Emery to the house.

TWELVE

E mery sat at the large kitchen table surrounded by grizzly bears, soaking in the happiness that flowed from the family. She was quiet at first, just listening, wishing she'd grown up with the kind of love and laughter they shared. What would it have been like to have her brothers care about her, and look out for her, just because they loved her? She would never know, because the cold, hard truth was that they didn't love her, and never really had. She'd been so naïve, until that fateful night that took her father from her. That night changed everything.

"You should have seen it, Emery! Nolan and Brayden came running around the barn like their clothes were on fire!" Briar was holding her stomach, tears streaming down her face as her laughter filled the room. "This little skunk was following close behind. Knox walked out of the barn yelling at them, wondering what the heck was going on, and then he just stopped. I was up in my room, safe in the house, and I saw the entire thing! That skunk sprayed the hell out of all three of them! It took us over a week to get the stench off them and out of the house."

"Come to find out, the skunk was a shifter Nolan managed to piss off the night before, from a bar in the next town over."

"Wait!" Emery interrupted, holding up a hand as she looked at all of them. "Are you telling me there are *skunk* shifters out there? Seriously?" When Miracle started giggling again, Emery shrugged, "What?"

"You learn something new every day," Noah said dryly.

"You guys are serious?" she muttered, looking at each one closely. There was no such thing as a skunk shifter, was there?

Nolan shook his head, standing and smacking Noah in the back of the head as he walked by. "No, they aren't. It was just a damn skunk. Trust me, I don't piss women off. I make them purr in enjoyment."

Briar spit her water across the table on a laugh, hitting the wooden surface with her hand. "Oh yeah, he makes them purr, all right! I don't think the grunting and groaning I heard coming from your bedroom a week ago had anything to do with purring!"

Emery's eyes widened, as she looked from Briar to Nolan, and back again. She heard Knox chuckle beside her, and then he reached over and began to idly play with a lock of her hair. "Was that what that was? I was wondering. I heard a crash, but was too tired to get up and check it out."

"I wasn't," Noah chimed in, taking a drink of his iced tea. "I opened his door to check on him. To this day, I

67

wish I had stayed in my own room. No matter how hard I try, I will never be able to unsee what I saw that night."

Nolan grinned, grabbing one of the homemade dinner rolls next to him, and throwing it at his brother. "Don't lie. You were taking notes, on the off chance that you get laid someday. You need to know what to do."

The friendly banter went on, and Emery tried to keep up, but it was hard. Half of the time, she couldn't tell if they were serious or not. Make that, most of the time.

"Would you like some more, Emery?"

Shaking herself out of her thoughts, Emery smiled over at Brayden as he came around the table to pick up her bowl. "No, thank you." When his face fell, she reached out and touched his arm, "It was very good. Did you make it?"

A low growl filled the room, and Brayden quickly stepped back, pulling away from her. Looking at Knox, he bared his neck in deference to his brother.

Crossing her arms over her chest, Emery raised an eyebrow, and snapped, "Really?" When Knox ignored her, she shook her head, and turned back to his sibling, asking again, "Did you make the soup?"

He nodded, a slow, boyish grin crossing his face. "Yep. I love to cook."

"Brayden's making ribs for dinner if you'd like to hang around," Miracle piped in. "You would love them!"

"I wish I could," Emery said, surprised to find that she really meant it, "but, I have to work tonight."

"What time?" Knox asked.

Glancing at her watch, she said, "I actually need to get going soon. I don't have to be at the Lyon's Den for a few hours, but I need to help Aurora with some things first."

"Aurora? The woman who lives just down the road?"

"Yes. I'm staying with her until... well, until I leave."

"What do you mean, until you leave?" Miracle asked softly. "Are you moving away from Moonstone?"

Another growl began to rumble around the room when Emery slowly nodded. "Yes, eventually. I don't have a choice."

"There is always a choice," Knox growled.

Laughing softly, even though there was nothing funny about her situation, Emery said, "You would get along great with Aurora. She seems to think the same thing."

"Maybe you should listen to her."

"I did," Emery murmured, raising a hand to brush it along his cheek. "That's why I'm here."

"But, you still plan on leaving." It wasn't a question.

Emery took a deep breath and looked around the room at his family. They all waited, watching her closely, as if hoping she would change her mind. But, she couldn't. Spending the past couple of hours with them had only proven to her that she needed to move on as soon as possible, for two reasons. The first one, was that she was in danger of falling for all of them, not just her mate. They were everything she had ever wanted in a family, and more. The second reason, was that she needed to do everything she could to ensure their safety. And, that wasn't being around her.

Standing, she held her head high even while her heart was breaking, as she told them, "I will stay as long as I can, but that's all I can promise. It isn't safe for me here, and it isn't safe for anyone around me. I can't put all of you in danger just so that I can find a piece of happiness." Leaning down, she lightly touched her lips to Knox's, before whispering, "I won't."

It was only after she left that Emery realized no one had really answered her question, one that was going to drive her crazy until she knew for sure. Did skunk shifters really exist?

CHAPTER
THIRTEEN

A week later, Knox waited out by Emery's truck for her to get off work. He could have gone inside, but after the way he'd acted the Saturday before when she touched his brother, he was afraid of how he would react if someone in the bar laid a hand on her. His parents had always warned him that grizzlies could be more possessive than other types of shifters, but he never knew exactly what they meant until he met Emery. After just a few days, he was already wanting to rip apart anyone who touched her soft, silky skin. Even his own family.

He needed to get control of his emotions, before he hurt someone. The only way to do that was to get her to spend some time with him. She'd been avoiding him since that day at his house. He'd tried to give her time to sort everything out, but that ended tonight. He missed her scent, her touch, the way her nose crinkled up when she laughed. He wanted to see her. Needed to.

When the back door opened, he smiled as Emery

stepped out. She tossed a trash bag into a dumpster in the alley, and then made her way toward him. "Hey," she whispered, stopping just in front of him, the top of her head barely reaching his chest. "What are you doing here?"

He shrugged, raising his hand to trail a finger down the side of her face. "Waiting for you."

Arching an eyebrow, she asked, "Are you keeping tabs on me, Channing?"

He grinned at the haughty tone. "Maybe."

"This isn't the first time either, is it?"

No, it wasn't. He came to the Lyon's Den nightly to see if she was working. If she was, he waited until her shift was over, and then followed her to Aurora's house at a distance.

"Maybe I just wanted to make sure you made it home okay."

"Oh, really?" Looking around, she asked, "Where's your car?"

"Truck."

"What?"

"I drive a truck," he muttered, sliding his fingers into her hair. "It's at the ranch. I had Nolan and Brayden drop me off on their way to the club earlier."

"Which club?" she whispered, a small catch in her voice. She was definitely affected by his touch, just as much as he was by hers.

"The Sexy Lyon." When her brow furrowed in confusion, he told her, "It's a strip club owned by Garrith's brother, Kendrix."

"Oh!" Her face flushed slightly as she whispered, "Do you go there, too?"

"Why would I, when I have everything I need right here?"

Emery shivered, leaning into him, "I meant, before you met me. Did you go then?"

"We just moved here a few weeks ago," Knox said, placing a soft kiss on her temple, and then moving down. "I've never been there." Tracing his tongue down her neck, he groaned when he reached the curve that would take him to where his mate mark belonged. He wanted to sink his teeth in deep, claiming her as his own, but he wouldn't do that without her permission. Unfortunately, it was obvious that she was nowhere near ready to give it.

"If you don't have your truck, how do you plan on getting back to your ranch?" she breathed, tilting her head to the side, giving him better access to the soft skin he was nuzzling.

"I was planning on having this cute little bunny shifter I picked up the other night drop me off on her way by," he rasped, nibbling his way back up her neck to tug on her earlobe with his teeth. "I was also hoping we could make a detour on the way, so I could show her a place I found about a week after we moved here. Somewhere I think she will really like."

"I suppose she would have to take you home," Emery whispered, slipping a hand under his shirt, and up over his chest. "Just to make sure you made it there safely."

Knox raked his teeth down her neck, reveling in the

moan that slipped free from her lips. "Can I show you my favorite place, Emery?"

Leaning back, she looked at him as she whispered, "Yes."

For what had to be the tenth time, Emery asked herself what she was doing. She knew exactly what was going to happen if she went somewhere alone with Knox Channing, but she didn't seem to have the energy to fight it. And, if she was honest, she just plain didn't want to.

"Turn here."

His deep, sexy voice sent a shiver of need through her, and she knew she was done trying to fight the inevitable. She had only lasted a week. Seven days. What did that say about her? She was weak. A fool. Hopeless.

Emery gasped when she stopped the truck in front of a large pond with a long, wooden dock leading out into the water. Trees surrounded the area, but the moon shone down on the water, lighting up the place. "It's beautiful."

Knox opened his door, and then came around the front of the truck to help her out. "I found it when I took one of the horses out for a ride," he said, guiding her down to the water, and out onto the pier.

"Is it on your land?"

"Yep. We own several acres. I like to explore when I have time."

As Emery stood at the end of the dock, gazing out over the softly rippling water, a feeling of peace washed over her. It was so quiet and calm. "How far are we from the main house?"

"Actually, no more than a mile. It's just back through the trees, so it can't be seen."

"A hidden secret," she whispered, raising her arms in the air and twirling around slowly. Tilting her head back to look at the moon, she smiled, "I love your favorite place, Knox. Thank you so much for sharing it with me."

"I love seeing you here," he whispered, taking a step closer to her.

Emery looked into dark eyes full of emotion and caved, giving in to what she'd wanted since the moment she first saw him. Moving closer to him, she dropped her hands to his chest, fisting his shirt and tugging until he lowered his head and captured her mouth with his. A small whimper left her throat when he traced her lips with his tongue, then slipped past them to find her own. She expected it to be hot and out of control like the other times he'd kissed her, but it wasn't. It was slow, sweet, and so much more.

Knox slid his hands under her shirt, and up her back holding her close. Emery moaned at the sensations flowing through her from the touch of his hands against her bare skin. She could feel the outline of his hard length against her, could sense the pent up desire in him, but still, he didn't lose control.

Moving his hips sensually against hers, he slowly raised his head and whispered, "I've missed you."

Her breath caught in her throat at his admission, and she reached up to place a hand on his cheek. "I've missed you, too." She had. Every single day. She knew part of it

75

was the fact that they hadn't completed the mate bond yet, but it was more than that. She genuinely liked him. From what she'd seen so far, he was a good man. Hard and unforgiving to those who harmed his family, but kind and gentle with the ones he cared about. Yes, he was gruff and possessive, and probably seemed overbearing to some, but not to her.

She'd been aware of the fact that he was there every night when she got off work, and that he followed her home, waiting until he knew she was in the house before continuing on to his ranch. It probably should have pissed her off, but it didn't. It made her feel safe and like someone actually gave a damn about her. Which was why she was here now, in his arms, with no plans to run... yet.

Leaning down, he nuzzled her cheek lightly as he whispered, "Come home with me."

She didn't have to think twice. "Yes."

FOURTEEN

When the truck stopped in front of his house, Knox lifted Emery's hand to his lips, placing a kiss in the center of her palm. "Emery, if you come in with me, there is no way in hell I'm going to be able to let you go."

She turned her pretty blue eyes his way and asked, "Were you ever going to?"

She had a point. "No," he admitted.

"Because I'm your mate," she whispered softly.

Cupping her cheek in his hand, Knox kissed her gently. "In the beginning."

"And now?"

"You are mine," he told her, tracing her cheek with his thumb, "but there's more to it, Emery. I care about you."

"You don't know me."

"I know enough."

Emery's eyes filled with tears, and she turned away from him, staring out the window next to her.

"I know you have a kind, gentle soul, even though you can handle your own if you need to. You are strong, and hate relying on others. You are scared of something, but don't want to pull others into whatever danger you are in. You were sweet to my sister when you didn't have to be. Kind to my brother when I was being an ass."

"Knox, there is so much about me that you don't know," Emery interjected.

"Then tell me."

Grasping his hand tightly, she said haltingly, "There are some very powerful people after me. They will be coming for me just as soon as they find out where I am. When they do, they will stop at nothing to take me back with them."

A slow anger filled him, and he growled, "No one is going to take you anywhere, Emery."

"If they find me, I may not have a choice," she whispered, lowering her head to look at their clasped hands. "That's why I can't stay in one place too long."

"How long have you been running?"

Raising tear-filled eyes to his, she said, "Less than a month. After I escaped, I came here. I don't want to go back, Knox."

He had no idea what she'd been through, no idea what was going on, but there was one thing he knew for certain. "You are not going anywhere, Emery. You are staying right here in Moonstone with me and my family. We will protect you. If anyone comes for you, it will be the last thing they do."

Emery let the tears slip free, unable to hold them back any longer. She had spent the past few weeks terrified, but determined not to return to her old herd no matter what she had to do. She was utterly exhausted, not only from lack of sleep, but also from stress and fear. She was so damn tired of being afraid.

"Hush, baby," Knox said gruffly, wiping the tears from her cheeks. "You aren't alone."

Kissing her gently, he was gone long enough to leave the truck and come around to her side. Opening the door, he gathered her in his arms, and slammed it shut with his foot. Emery was vaguely aware of entering his home, going up a set of stairs, and then soon after, she was placed on a soft bed.

Knox removed her shoes first, then went over to his dresser and took out a burgundy tee-shirt. She watched as he quickly took off his clothes, all except for a pair of black boxer briefs that hugged his hard cock snuggly. Crossing the room to her, he placed a knee on the bed. "Come here, sweet bunny," he said softly, helping her sit up before gently removing her long-sleeved shirt and bra and tossing them to the chair in the corner. Slipping his own shirt over her head, he placed a soft kiss on her lips, and guided her back down onto the pillow.

Emery moaned when his hands slid down her body, stopping at the top of her jeans. Slowly, he unbuttoned them, and then slipped them down her legs and off. Throwing them in the direction of the chair, he laid down next to her, cupping her face in the palm of his large hand. "Get some sleep, baby."

Her eyes widened when she realized that he planned

on going no further. Fuck that. She wanted him, needed him, and she wasn't waiting any longer. Shoving hard on his shoulder, she laughed at the surprise in his eyes when he fell back on the bed and she straddled him, her hot, wet pussy against his straining cock. "Later," she murmured, running her hands down his chest.

"I thought..."

"You thought what?" she asked, moving her hips against him.

"Fuck, baby, you gotta stop that!"

"Why?"

"This is supposed to be about you," he said, grasping her hips tightly, and pushing up into her. "You need rest. Time. Sleep."

Gripping the top of his underwear in her hands, she shook her head. "That can wait, Knox. Right now, I need you."

Knox groaned, lifting up slightly so that she could slide the briefs down over his thighs and off, dropping them to the floor. "Emery, I'm trying to do what's best for you."

"I know what is best for me," she whispered, sliding back up his body, but stopping just over his long, thick cock that was begging for her attention. "Let me worry about that, right now."

Leaning forward, she licked the tip of his dick, and Knox groaned loudly as his hips jerked in reaction. "Emery, we need to talk," he rasped.

"I'm done talking." Wrapping her hand around the base of his cock, she twirled her tongue around the head, and then swallowed him down.

"Jesus Christ!" Knox roared, clutching tightly to the covers at his side as he pushed up into her mouth. "Baby, that feels so fucking good!"

Emery grinned around his dick, and then began to slide slowly up and down the rock-hard shaft, taking him deeper and deeper.

"Emery! You have to stop. I'm going to come!"

There was no way in hell she was stopping. She wanted to make him come. Wanted to feel the power it would give her, knowing she'd been able to set her mate on fire. Sucking him deep, she pulled back and flicked her tongue over the underside of the head, and then engulfed him again. Cupping his balls in her hand, she did that three more times before he shouted her name, filling her mouth like he'd promised.

She took it all, reveling in his taste, and then, when she was sure he was done, she slid up his body and straddled his waist. Leaning down, she rested her arms on his chest, and placed her chin on her folded hands. A satisfied smile crossed her lips as she purred, "See, I feel better already. I knew exactly what I needed."

Knox's eyes darkened, and he growled, "That was fantastic, but you don't think we are done, do you?"

"What?" Emery frowned in confusion, and then let out a small squeak when he grabbed her hips and moved her up to his chest. With a naughty grin, he held up a hand and let his large claws spring free. Slipping one in the neckline of his shirt, he yanked it down, effectively stripping the material from her body.

"It's your turn."

Emery gasped when he slid a claw inside the

81

waistband of her panties, and sliced them open, first on one side, then the other. She raised up slightly, and shuddered when he stripped them from her. "Oh, God," she panted, waiting in anticipation to see what he was going to do next. She didn't have to wait long.

"I've been wanting to taste you from the moment we met," he growled, filling her with excitement, and causing the juices to flow from her pussy. His claws retracted, and he slid his hand over to her stomach and down her belly, stopping just above the part of her that ached to feel his touch. "You are mine, Emery," he growled softly. "No one is going take you from me. Not ever. That's a promise."

Before she could respond, he moved his hand lower, dipping his thumb in between her wet lips, and then bringing it up to caress her throbbing clit. She cried out as he rubbed the aching nub in circles, shudders running through her body. It felt so good, better than anyone else's touch ever had before. "Please, Knox. Please."

His eyes hot with fire, he stopped, bringing his thumb to his mouth and licking her cream from it. Snarling, he grasped her hips and lifted her up, until his tongue found her folds, lapping at the juices. "Mine," he growled, licking at her. "Mine!"

"Yours," she cried, moving her hips in pleasure. "All yours, Knox."

Knox licked her clit, flicking his tongue quickly back and forth, and she screamed as her orgasm came out of nowhere. It was long and hard, and throughout the entire thing, Knox continued to lick her. When she was done, he finally stopped, letting her slide down in his arms. "Tastes like honey," he muttered, licking his lips. "So fucking good."

Emery fought to control her breathing, clutching at the mat of hair on his chest. It was thick and soft, and she loved it. "Are we done now?" she whispered, already knowing the answer at the way his hard cock was rubbing up against her bottom.

"Not even close."

Her hands on his chest, she pushed up on her arms and looked at him. "Good."

Backing up slightly, she arched her hips and reached back to grab his cock in her hand. Slowly, she lowered herself onto it, moaning as he filled her. She had to pause halfway down and wait until she adjusted to his size, and then she lowered herself all of the way onto him. A low growl rumbled through Knox's chest, and she gasped when she looked up to see his eyes flashing bear, and his fangs had punched through his gums. She could feel his claws pinching the skin on her hips as he clutched her tightly.

"Knox." She breathed his name as she watched his eyes go to her shoulder, and she saw him struggle not to rear up and bite her. Her bunny responded, and before she knew it, her own fangs were showing, along with her claws. Scraping them over the hair on his chest, Emery moaned as she began to move. Slowly at first, and then faster and faster. He felt so good inside her, stretching her with his thickness, sending shivers throughout her body.

"You feel so good," Knox growled, moving deep inside her. "So hot and wet. So tight."

"Knox!" The pleasure was building quickly, and she was racing toward it. There was no holding back. She met him thrust for thrust, digging her nails into his chest.

"Come with me," Knox ordered, groaning loudly as he pushed into her. "So close."

"Yes," she cried as her body tensed up, and then she came on him.

A loud roar ripped from his chest as Knox slammed into her one last time. He threw his head back, his teeth bared as he stared at the junction between her neck and shoulder, where he wanted to leave his mark. She tilted her head to the side, and waited for the inevitable, but it never came.

Breathing heavily, Emery collapsed against his chest, circling her arm up around his neck as she whispered, "You didn't bite me."

Knox was quiet for a moment, struggling to catch his breath, too. Running a hand gently down her back, he said, "You aren't ready for that, Emery."

"I'm sorry."

"Don't be. When I make you mine, I want you all in. Until then, this works just fine."

He was right, she wasn't ready. But, she wanted to be. Swallowing hard, she decided to give him something, the way he had her, by waiting for her to make the choice on her own. "Knox?"

"Yeah, baby?"

"My name isn't really Emery."

FIFTEEN

E mery woke the next morning to the sound of laughter and smell of bacon. Raising her arms, she stretched, groaning softly at the subtle aches in her body. She and Knox had talked for a while after her revelation the night before, but he didn't press her for answers, knowing she wasn't ready to give them. Instead, he told her about his parents, and the car accident that took them over six months ago. It was obvious that he loved them very much, just as he did the rest of his family. As far as he knew, they were the last of the Channing bloodline. His father was raised with a sister and a brother, but the sister passed away over ten years ago, and the brother moved away when he was just eighteen. The news of his death had come just five years later.

Knox became the head of the family, and was now responsible for all of his siblings. Granted, they were adults, but it didn't matter. They were unmated, and his to look out for. He took that seriously. She may have only met the man a week ago, but a part of her knew that she could trust him with her life. The thought of leaving Moonstone was moving further and further from her mind, covered by ones of staying instead, and having a mate, along with a family who she could easily learn to love.

At the sound of Miracle's laughter, Emery rose, searching for her jeans. Slipping them on, she decided to forego her own shirt, and found a new one of Knox's in his dresser. She put it on, and then stood for a moment huddled in it, soaking in his scent. Closing her eyes, she sighed, wishing she could wake up like this every day.

The sound of more laughter, and her stomach growling, got Emery moving again. After making quick use of the bathroom, and the toothpaste she found in one of the drawers under the sink, she left Knox's bedroom and made her way down to the kitchen.

Standing in the doorway, Emery watched Knox with his family, a strange warmth filling her at the sight of their happiness. She could be a part of this. When Knox looked up from where he sat at the head of the table and held out his arm to her, she realized she already *was* a part of it. She was his mate, even if they hadn't completed the bond yet, which meant his family accepted her presence in his life, and in theirs.

Crossing the room, she ignored his brothers and sisters, and slipped into his lap, wrapping her arms around his neck. "Good morning."

His eyes darkened, and he leaned close. "Morning, baby." Sliding his hand up through her hair, he cupped the back of her head, holding her still as he captured her lips with his.

Emery sighed, leaning into his kiss, loving the feel of him holding her close. Knox nipped at her lower lip, soothing the sting with his tongue, before doing it again. A moan slipped free before she could stop it, and she felt the hard length of him pressing against her bottom.

"No one better say another word about me bringing women here after what we had to listen to last night," Nolan said, placing a plate of bacon down on the table.

Knox growled low in warning, but Emery just laughed against his lips. Turning to look at his brother, she cocked an eyebrow and said, "From what it sounded like, you were doing more than making a little noise. Something about breaking things?"

"A little noise?" Briar piped up. "Is that what you call it?"

"Well, you have some great, pound-on-the-wall sex, and try to keep it down,"

"Pound-on-the-wall sex?" Miracle asked, looking around the room.

"Yeah, you know, the sex is so good that you have to pound on the wall while you are having it."

The room was quiet as everyone stared at her, and then Brayden burst into laughter. "Is that what that was?"

"Shush, woman," Knox said, nipping at her playfully as he chuckled.

The doorbell rang as Emery leaned in to give Knox a kiss. This was how it should be. She wanted this, all of it, for the rest of her life.

"There you are!" a female voice said, and Emery's head snapped around as a woman walked into the room, her blue eyes twinkling, a huge smile on her face. She held a bright yellow gift bag in one hand, and she came around the table to set it down in front of them. "I'm so glad you're both here! I'd heard a rumor that you found your mate, Knox Channing, and I wanted to drop by with a small present for the two of you."

A present? Emery looked around the room in confusion, before bringing her gaze back to the woman. "I'm sorry. I don't think we've met?'

"Not yet, my dear." Holding out her hand, she smiled, "My name is Hollie Lyons."

"Oh! You're Garrith's mother!" She was also mated to Leo Lyons, the alpha of Moonstone.

"Yes, I am. And, it is very nice to meet you. I'm so glad one of our bears has found his mate." Her bears? Emery turned to look at Knox, but he just shook his head, watching Hollie in amusement. "Now, open your present before I leave. I'm running late. I'm supposed to watch the twins today so Garrith and Tatum can have some alone time. They don't get that very often lately."

"Of course," Emery said, moving to get off Knox's lap.

"Please, stay where you are. It makes my heart happy to see young love."

Ignoring the remark about love, Emery shifted and pulled the bag closer. "If you're sure?"

"Of course! Now, open it. I had so much fun picking your gifts out."

As the woman's eyes lit with excitement, and something else Emery couldn't decipher, she untied the bow at the top and peered inside. Her cheeks darkened to a deep red, and she immediately slammed the bag shut again. "Um, thank you so much for the present, Mrs. Lyons, but I think it would be better if Knox and I opened it alone."

"Nonsense! I want to watch you! Now, come on, Emery," she said, clapping her hands, "hurry up."

"What is it?" Knox whispered in her ear.

Glancing over at him, she took a deep breath, and reached into the bag to pull out a hot pink lace teddy. Holding it up for him to see, she giggled when he grunted, "Oh..."

"Wow! That's hot," Nolan said, reaching over to touch it.

Knox slapped his hand away, grabbing the teddy himself. "Find your own damn mate, and then you can touch her under things," he snarled.

"Under things?" Briar gasped, laughing so hard tears appeared. "Come on, big brother, you can say it. It's a negligée."

"A negla what?"

Miracle giggled, "A negligée. A teddy. A nightie."

"Well, whatever the hell it is, no one needs to be touching it but me," Knox snapped.

Shaking her head, Emery reached into the bag and pulled out a tube of lube, handing it to Knox, who frowned in confusion. Then she pulled out... nipple clamps.

"Those can be a lot of fun, from what I hear," Hollie said, reaching over to take them from her. "You just open them and hook them onto your..."

"I can figure it out," Emery promised, interrupting

the woman as her mate's face turned a darker shade of red than her own.

"Damn! Can I borrow those later?" Nolan asked. "I bet Gina from the club would love them."

"She already has a pair of her own," Brayden said, taking a drink of his milk. "I saw them a couple of weeks ago."

"Well, crap. Maybe Cindy would like them."

"Nolan." Knox growled his name in warning.

Emery looked over to where Hollie was watching her expectantly, and knew she better keep going so that she didn't insult the woman. Taking a deep breath, she reached back into the bag, and pulled out a large, hot pink dildo. "It matched the teddy," Hollie said in excitement. "I had to get it for you."

Emery went through what was left in the bag, from flavored lotions to anal beads, wishing she could crawl into a hole somewhere and hide. Finally, she reached the last item. A pair of bright red edible underwear. Her face on fire, she stuttered out a thank you to Hollie while Noah choked on his laughter from where he stood by the counter.

"You are very welcome! Congratulations again on your mating, and if you ever need anything, you just let us know."

"We will," Emery promised, as she slowly placed each item back in the bag. "You have a good day with your grandbabies."

As soon as Hollie was gone, Knox stood, lifting Emery in his arms. "Knox! What are you doing?"

"Grab the damn bag!" he ordered, waiting until she did, and then stalking from the room.

"Knox?"

He cleared the stairs in record time, and soon they were in his room, the door slamming shut behind him. His eyes glowed a bright brown as he growled, "You can't expect me to sit down there with my brothers and sisters when I am hard as a fucking rock thinking about you in that pink thing, can you?"

Emery squealed when he tossed her onto the bed, immediately following behind her. Her breath left her when he crawled up and over her, a growl rumbling deep in his throat. "No," she whispered, a low moan leaving her throat when he leaned down and sucked her nipple into his mouth, shirt and all.

"Good," Knox muttered, rolling over onto his back, his arm behind his head. Reaching down, he undid the snap on his jeans, and pulled the zipper down, freeing his cock. Fisting it in his hand, he growled, "Now go put that nightie, teddy thing on and come ride me, woman."

Emery scrambled off the bed, grabbing the bag and quickly finding the teddy. She was only too happy to oblige.

SIXTEEN

"I'm going to tell him."

Aurora raised her eyes from the flowers she was busy planting and glanced over at her. "It affects more than just him."

"I know."

The last three weeks had gone by in a blur. When she wasn't working, she was with Knox and his family. She insisted on living at Aurora's, even though she kept coming home later and later each night. She had begun to wonder why she was fighting it so hard. A part of her was still afraid of what would happen when her brother and Alpha Ramsey found her, and there was no doubt in her mind that they would if she stayed in Moonstone, but that fear wasn't enough to make her leave. She was finding out that she had so much more to stay for.

Emery knelt beside the woman, smiling at her. Aurora had become more than just her savior since her rescue. She was her friend, and it was a friendship Emery did not take lightly. She wouldn't be here today if it weren't for her. She wouldn't know what it was like to be free of her family, to make her own decisions, to have the chance to fall in love with a gruff, but adorable, grizzly bear. She also wouldn't know what it was like to have someone she could confide in about her fears, like she knew she could with Aurora. "I'm going to tell them all. It's the right thing to do."

Setting the flower down that she held, Aurora reached over to grasp Emery's hand in her own. "Does this mean you are staying in Moonstone?"

Taking a deep breath, Emery nodded. "These past few weeks with Knox have been the best of my life, Aurora. He is everything to me, and his family treats me as if I am one of them."

"Because you are," Aurora whispered, squeezing her hand tightly. "As Knox's mate, you are a part of their family."

"We haven't completed the mate bond," Emery said, looking out over the farm. "He refuses to until I'm ready."

"It looks to me like you are ready now." Standing, Aurora tugged on her hand until Emery rose, too. "Let's go."

Emery's eyes misted with tears as she looked at her friend. "You're coming with me?"

"Of course." A soft smile curved Aurora's lips as she said, "I knew from the moment you arrived that there were two different paths you could follow on your journey, Emery. I was praying this was the one you would choose."

Emery didn't question the other woman. The gifts

Aurora had were powerful, and after living with her for a couple of months now, she'd learned to just accept them. "Aurora, can you see what's going to happen? I mean, have you seen me in the future? Was I happy?"

Aurora hugged her tightly, and whispered, "All I can tell you, is that we are going to fight like hell to make sure you are."

"We?"

Leaning back, Aurora's green eyes sparkled with emotion as she whispered, "We are in this together, my friend. To the end."

Knox brushed down the gelding's coat, speaking softly to him. He'd just gotten back from a long ride, and was in a hurry to finish so he could shower and go pick up Emery. It was finally warming up, and they had plans for a picnic at their favorite spot. They'd been there several times since he first showed it to her, and he was even contemplating building a small cabin beside the pond, as a little getaway from the main house. He might even share it with his brothers and sisters, if they were lucky. As much as they loved each other, sometimes it was nice to get away for a while.

At the sound of a vehicle in the driveway, he glanced out the barn door to see a silver four-door car stop in front of the house. As he watched, a tall woman with long, red hair emerged from the driver's side, and Emery from the passenger. The redhead said something to

Emery, who nodded and then made her way to the house, while the other woman turned toward him.

Knox waited patiently for her to enter the barn, instinctively knowing who she was, even though they hadn't officially met, yet. "Aurora."

She nodded, a solemn look on her face. "It's nice to finally meet you, Knox."

"You've lived next to us for months, but never bothered to stop by. You didn't even respond when my sisters left you an invitation for dinner. Twice. What are you doing here now?"

Sighing, Aurora ran her fingers through her hair and grimaced. "I apologize for my rudeness. I just know how this is all going to play out, so I've been putting our meeting off as long as possible."

Raising his eyebrows, Knox asked, "Why do I get the feeling that you aren't talking about you and me?"

"Because, I'm not." Gesturing toward the gelding, she said, "Why don't you put him away and come inside? Emery has something she wants to talk to you and your family about."

"And you're here for moral support?"

"I'm here because my friend needs me, Knox."

CHAPTER

SEVENTEEN

Emery waited in the kitchen for Knox, listening idly to the way his brothers and sisters teased each other. As soon as she and Aurora arrived, she had gone into the house to get everyone together. They didn't ask questions when she told them she needed to talk to them, just gathered around the kitchen table where they always preferred to talk as a group.

Everyone grew quiet when Knox entered the kitchen, followed by Aurora. Emery's eyes widened in surprise when a low growl filled the room, and her gaze swung to Knox's brother. Noah stared at Aurora, his eyes darkening as he pushed his chair back from the table.

Aurora held up a hand, shaking her head. "Not now, fur ball. We have other things to worry about."

"So, this is why you have been avoiding us," Knox said dryly, crossing the room to take his place at the head of the table.

Ignoring him, Aurora came to stand beside Emery, slipping a hand into hers in encouragement. "Emery

96

needs you all right now, so please, let's make this about her."

"Why didn't you tell me?" Emery whispered, pulling her gaze from Noah to look at her friend.

"Because, this is about you, Emery. Not me."

"But, you said having a mate is a blessing."

"It is."

"You told me to fight for what I want. That if you had a mate..."

"Emery, stop. Please."

"You're my friend, Aurora. You could have talked to me."

"And, I will. Just not right now."

"Emery," Knox interrupted, holding out his hand to her, "Aurora said you have something to tell us?"

Emery nodded, straightening her shoulders, but staying where she was. There was no way she could get through the story without crying if she went to her mate. "Yes, I do."

The room fell quiet, even Noah's growling was silenced, as the Channing family looked at her expectantly. She smiled at them one-by-one, before letting go of Aurora's hand. Stepping forward, she raised her head high as she said, "First of all, I want to apologize to all of you."

"You have nothing to apologize for, Emery," Aurora interjected. "None of this is your fault. You've done nothing wrong, and they will see that as soon as you explain."

Swallowing hard, Emery shook her head, "I lied to them."

Aurora placed her hands on her hips, her green eyes snapping, "You did it to survive, Emery Ericksen. Don't you ever forget that. You are a fighter."

"Emery, we all love you no matter what," Miracle said quietly. "Nothing you tell us now is going to change that."

"She's right," Knox growled. "Just tell us what is going on, so we can figure out how to protect you from whatever is coming our way."

Emery looked at her family, because that was what they were, and a tremulous smile crossed her lips. "I am so grateful for each and every one of you. Especially you, Aurora. I probably wouldn't even be alive if it weren't for you."

"What the fuck is she talking about?" Noah demanded, and Emery's eyes widened when she saw the tips of his fangs peeking out from his mouth. In all the time she'd known him, he'd never lost control.

"My real name isn't Emery," Emery said softly, crossing her arms over her chest, and holding herself tightly. "It's Princess Lena Remmington."

"Princess?" Briar gasped.

Chuckling, Emery shook her head, "No, I'm not exactly royalty. Princess is the name my father gave me when I was born, because I was his only daughter. I was his princess." Shaking her head, Emery swiped at a tear that ran down her cheek. "My dad was also the alpha of our herd, so I was considered the princess to all of my people. Unfortunately, that didn't mean much when he died, and my brother took over."

"What happened after your brother became alpha?" Brayden asked quietly.

"At first, nothing. Samson was too busy with his new duties to even look my way. My mother had always been jealous of my relationship with my father. She just continued to ignore me like she had most of my life. My other two brothers did the same. Then, things changed."

"Why?" Miracle asked, when Emery paused to collect her thoughts.

"Because Samson decided it was time I took a mate, and he basically sold me off to the highest bidder."

"What the fuck?" Knox snarled, slamming a fist onto the table.

"I think it all started because I was looking into my father's death more closely," Emery admitted. "The whole thing never made sense to me. We were told it was a hunting accident, but nothing else. I wasn't allowed to see my father's body," she whispered, another tear slipping free. "Nobody was, until the night of the ceremony to send his spirit on to the afterworld. Even then, we weren't allowed close. My brothers carried him to a pyre they'd built just outside our village and laid him on it. Then, a couple of people said some words, they lit it, and he was gone."

"There's more," Aurora said, cocking an eyebrow.

Emery nodded, "Yes." Her gaze going slowly around the room, she told them, "I snuck into the small shack where they were keeping his body just hours before the ritual. I had to see him one last time." Wiping at tears, she rasped, "There were bite marks and dark bruises all over his body. It was horrible! There was no way it was a hunting accident. It looked as if he was mauled to death. And, the stench of coyote was all over him."

"So, he was attacked by coyotes?" Nolan asked in confusion. "Why wouldn't your brothers just tell everyone that?"

"Because," Emery whispered, trembling as she told them, "I know this is a huge accusation, but I seriously think they had him killed."

"Jesus," Brayden breathed, leaning forward in his seat. "What kind of person kills his own family?"

"Just two weeks after my father's death, I was told I was to mate with Alpha Ramsey," Emery told them. "He has a herd not too far from ours. I found out not long ago from Aurora, that he has an alliance with a coyote pack."

"Son of a bitch," Knox snarled.

"I refused to bond with him. I told Samson there was no way he could make me, but my brother wouldn't take no for an answer. The next thing I knew, I was stuck in a room in the basement that was more like a prison cell than a room. It had cement walls on all sides, and the door had a window with bars. There was a small bathroom in the corner, a cot, and not much else. Samson and my other brothers would come down daily and take turns at me with their fists. It was mostly Samson, but Frederick and Hamilton were in on it, too. I was given very small rations of food, if any at all. I was so hungry."

"They were trying to break you," Brayden muttered, his voice deep with anger, something she'd never heard from the man before.

"Yes," Emery agreed, bowing her head for a moment

as the memories swamped her. "They thought I would give in and agree to mate with Alpha Ramsey. One time, my mother came to see me. I was so sure she was there to set me free. I don't know why I thought after all of these years that she gave a damn about me. Instead, she told me that I was to mate with Ramsey. I didn't have a choice. He would be there in two days, and if I didn't follow through with it, I would be killed."

"Oh, Emery," Miracle whispered, with tears in her eyes and despair in her voice. "I can't imagine everything you went through."

"How did you escape?" Noah asked, his eyes solely on her now.

"After Alpha Ramsey arrived, they brought him down to meet me." Emery glanced over at Aurora, before saying, "His daughter, Meadow, was with him. I was told that we were to have the mating ceremony the next night after a dinner celebration. When I told him what I thought of that, he hit me hard enough that I blacked out. Later that night, I heard Meadow's voice outside the door. She told me that she was going to get me out of there, and to be ready the next night for more instructions. When she came back the next time, she had somehow gotten ahold of one of the keys to my cell. Before I knew what was happening, I was free, and she was telling me to run as fast as I could to the falls without looking back. That someone would be waiting for me at the bottom of them."

"That someone was you," Noah said quietly, glancing at Aurora.

"Yes."

"Meadow and Aurora rescued me. They saved my life. If it wasn't for them, I would be dead right now, because there was no way I was mating that bastard. He's a cruel, heartless, son of a bitch. His daughter has to live in hell every day of her life."

"I told you, it's her choice, Emery," Aurora said. "I've tried to help her. She refuses."

"He's going to find out someday that she is the one helping all of these people escape, Aurora," Emery snapped, anger filling her at the thought of what would happen to the girl when he did. "She's innocent, sweet, kind, and the night that she freed me, she was terrified. I could smell it on her. I can't leave her there. I just can't!"

"Brave," Briar said.

"What?"

"You forgot brave. She might be scared, but she is very courageous putting all of those lives before her own."

"And you help her?" Noah asked Aurora, grimacing slightly as he said it.

"Yes," Aurora snapped, her eyes lit with fire, "I help her. Every damn time she calls, I help her. Because it is what I am on this earth to do. It is my calling, and I am not going to stop any more than Meadow is."

"Even though you are scared every time, too," Emery whispered, suddenly understanding what it must cost her friend when she put her life on the line to save others the way she did.

"Yes," Aurora admitted through gritted teeth. "If it weren't for people like myself and Meadow, people willing to stand up against the violence and corruption in this world, we would lose a lot of very special individuals. I'm not willing to let that happen."

"Right now," Knox interrupted, leveling his gaze on Aurora, "I'm not worried about this Meadow person, or your little side gig saving people who find themselves in unfortunate situations." His eyes moving to his siblings, and then Emery, he thundered, "Right now, I am worried about my mate! What can we expect from her family and this alpha? How close are they to finding her?"

Aurora hesitated, before replying, "I've had eyes on them ever since I brought Emery to Moonstone. They haven't found her yet, Knox, but they are close. Very close."

"What are we up against?" Nolan asked, a guarded look entering his eyes.

"Let's just say, I've called my coven home to help."

"All of them?" Emery squeaked in surprise.

"Coven?" Several others questioned.

"You have got to be fucking kidding me," Noah grunted, shaking his head in disgust, a look of contempt on his features.

"All of them," Aurora said quietly. "We are going to need them." Turning to Knox, she whispered, "And, that is why I stayed away up until now. Not because I knew my mate was here, but because I know he will never be able to accept me for who I am. A witch."

EIGHTEEN

L ater that night, Knox laid in bed holding Emery tightly in his arms. He'd spent most of the day with his brothers, trying to formulate a plan to keep her safe. They needed to be alert and ready for anything, because there was no doubt in his mind that her brothers and Alpha Ramsey were coming for her. If Aurora said it was going to happen, then it would. He and his family had dealt with witches in the past, and from his own personal experience, the ones who had the gift of sight were never wrong.

"I'm so sorry I brought all of this trouble to your door, Knox."

Putting a finger under her chin, he tilted her head up until her gaze met his. "I'm not. Baby, my life is complete now that you are in it. You are everything to me. You own me, heart and soul. Everything else will work itself out, one way or another."

"I can't believe you still want me," she whispered,

slipping her arms around his neck and burrowing closer to him.

"Why wouldn't I?"

"Because, I'm bringing death to your door, Knox," she cried, burying her face in his neck. "They will kill whoever gets in their way."

Cupping the back of her head, he slid his fingers through the thick strands of her hair and tugged. When she finally looked at him, he grunted, "Emery, I'm a fucking bear. They are rabbits. How do you really think this scenario is going to work out?"

She paused, her mouth forming a perfect 'O', before a slow smile crossed her face. "Bears eat rabbits."

"Damn right, they do," he muttered, nuzzling her cheek with his own. "Now, do I need to remind you how this bear eats his bunny?"

A giggle escaped, and Emery moved the lower half of her body against his, making his cock stand to attention. "You know, I think I might have forgotten. Maybe you should show me again."

Growling playfully, Knox turned her over on her back, covering her body with his. Brushing her hair back from her face, he whispered, "We are going to get through this, my beautiful mate. You are my world, and I promise, I will keep you safe."

She stared at him in silence for a moment, and then whispered, "Knox?"

"Yeah, baby?" he rasped, breathing in her scent before lowering his head to run his tongue over her bare shoulder and up the side of her neck. She was blissfully naked underneath him, and he was ready to take advantage of that.

"Bite me."

Knox froze, instantly going rock-hard as his fangs punched through his gums. "Emery, are you sure?"

"I've never been more sure of anything in my life," she whispered, right before she sank her sharp teeth into his shoulder.

With a loud shout, he reciprocated, his own fangs finding the soft skin where he'd imagined placing his mark for several weeks now. Fisting his cock, he found her wet heat and slid deep inside, pumping his hips fast and hard as he came quickly, roaring in pleasure against her shoulder. He felt her own orgasm hit, her pussy clamping down on his cock, milking everything he had from him.

Bracing himself on his forearms, he slowly removed his fangs and licked at his bite, sealing it with saliva, before raising his head to look at her. She was watching him through heavy lidded eyes, licking drops of his blood from her lips. She was the most beautiful sight he'd ever seen. "Mine," he rasped thickly through his huge fangs. "Mine."

"Yours," she agreed, rising up to kiss him gently, before falling back to the pillow. "I love you, my mate," she whispered, before succumbing to her exhaustion.

Trailing soft kisses from her temple to her chin, he gathered her in his arms and rolled over onto his back, resting her against him. Tugging the covers over them, he closed his eyes, holding her tightly. "I love you, sweet bunny."

NINETEEN

Emery slowly made her way around the bar filling drinks, taking away dirty glasses, and cleaning tables. It was early evening, but she'd been there since they opened, and she was ready to be off her aching feet. Knox was outside with his brothers, waiting to take her home. They'd decided it was best if at least one of them was with her at all times, so Knox came to the bar with her for the first couple of hours she was there, then Nolan showed up, quickly followed by Brayden and Noah when they got off work. Right now, they had the building surrounded, making sure no one unusual entered who could be a threat to her.

As much as she wanted to tell them they were smothering her, she couldn't, because she knew they did what they did out of love. She finally had the older brothers she'd always wanted, and a mate who meant everything to her.

"You ever gonna get me another drink, girl?"

Emery froze when her wrist was encircled by a rough

hand, and her gaze flew to the wolf in front of her. Cyrus. She'd stupidly forgotten about him while she was daydreaming, a mistake she shouldn't have made. "As soon as you get your paws off of me," she snapped, yanking hard as she tried to free herself from his tight grip.

"I'm not so sure I want to do that."

Fear filled her, but she refused to give in to it. "I don't really care what you want. Let go of me, now!"

"There's a bounty on your head, Princess," Cyrus said quietly, his eyes gleaming in the dim light. "I aim to collect it. They should be here soon for you."

Son of a bitch. They'd found her. Not thinking twice, Emery dropped the tray she held, and glass shattered all over the floor. Bringing her knee up, she slammed it into Cyrus's crotch, and then turned and fled. She heard Cale yelling behind her, but she kept going, down the hall and out the back door where she knew she would find Knox.

The minute she cleared the door, he was there, pulling her close. "Talk to me, baby. What happened?"

"Emery, are you okay?"

She heard Cale's voice, but was shaking so bad she couldn't answer.

"Emery? What the hell is going on? I think you just gave that weasel, Cyrus, a sex change. Not that I'm complaining, but damn, girl!" Tatum yelled from behind Cale, but Emery couldn't find her voice to respond.

"Emery?" Knox held her gently, waiting patiently for her to look at him before asking, "What happened?" His tone was cool and calm, but his eyes were a different story. He was ready to go find the wolf and tear him apart. The only thing keeping him there was her.

"They found me, Knox," she whispered, shaking her head in denial. "He called me Princess. Said there is a bounty on my head, and he was going to collect the money. They will be here soon for me."

"Does someone want to tell me what the hell is going on?" Garrith Lyons demanded from the open doorway. "Do I need to get the sheriff over here so you can press charges against Cyrus, Emery? Did he hurt you?"

Tatum laughed, a snort slipping free, "She deballed the bastard already, cat. I think it's taken care of."

"Deballed?"

"Ya know, kneed him so hard in the cojones that he is going to be singing soprano for a week. Might never have kids again. Totally lost his man card, that's for sure."

"Jesus, woman!"

"My mate is being hunted by her family," Knox said, interrupting them. "And also by the alpha they tried to sell her to."

"What the hell?" Tatum yelled, placing her hands on her hips. "You mean to tell me, they tried to sell her off like a fucking object?"

"Tatum..."

"No! No one messes with my friends, Garrith Lyons. You should know that by now!" Her eyes glowing with anger, she snarled, "Now, you go get all your furry friends, and you help her, or I will!"

Shaking his head in exasperation, Garrith ignored his mate and looked at Knox. "What are we looking at?"

Emery leaned into her bear, soaking up his strength

as he replied, "Well, let me put it to you this way. Right now, we have nine witches on their way here to help protect Emery."

"Shit."

"Yeah."

"We need to get Emery home, Knox," Nolan said, rounding the corner of the building. "We can't keep her safe out here, and we can't risk anyone in town getting hurt."

"Take her back to your ranch, Knox. I will gather my pride, and we will be there soon."

Emery looked over at him in surprise, clutching tightly to Knox's shirt as she fought for the courage to face what was to come. "You are going to help me?"

"Emery," Garrith said kindly, walking over to place a gentle hand on her shoulder, "you've worked here for how long now? At least three months. You've been in this town for even longer. Hell, my mother came to visit you at Knox's place. She claimed you as one of her own. You are family now. Pride. Of course, we are going to help."

"We need to move, Knox!" Noah called from the end of the alley. "Briar caught word that Emery's brothers will be here soon. And they aren't alone."

"Caught word?" Emery asked in confusion. "How did she do that?"

"You'd be surprised what my sister can do with that computer of hers," Knox told her, his voice hard, his face a cold mask. "Let's go."

CHAPTER
TWENTY

When they reached the ranch, Briar was waiting out front, and Emery's eyes widened when she saw a gun strapped to her thigh and another at her waist.

"We need to hurry. That scumbag, Cyrus, told the bastards exactly where to find Emery. Seems like he's been watching her for a while now," Briar told them as soon as they exited their vehicles.

"Where's Miracle?" Knox demanded, stalking past her and heading for the house, his hand on Emery's back as he brought her with him.

"I'm right here."

Emery raised her head and gasped when she saw that Knox's sweet, little sister was strapping, too.

"Dammit, Miracle, you need to get into the safe room. Now!"

"Not going to happen," Miracle said, turning on her heel and going back into the house.

"I can't keep an eye on you out there, sis. I won't be able to keep you safe."

Miracle turned around abruptly, her hands on her hips, her eyes flashing, as she growled fiercely, "I do *not* need you to protect me, Knox Channing! You worry about your mate, not me. I can handle myself."

"While that may have been true in the past, things have changed," Noah said gently, as he stepped around Knox to make his way toward Miracle. "You've been through so much, Miracle. You might freeze up out there. If we are focused on you, it could get someone else hurt."

"If you expect me to stand down when my sister is being threatened, you better think again," Miracle snarled, her clear blue eyes sparkling, shining bright as sapphires. "No one is taking Emery from us. I don't give a damn who they are! Now, stop wasting your time trying to change my mind, and gear up! They are going to be here anytime, and we need to be ready."

"Gear up?" Emery whispered, shock filling her at the difference in the woman who stood in front of her. Gone, was the meek and mild Miracle she knew. In her place, stood a fierce warrior who was ready to stand against an army for her. "Sister?" Emery swallowed hard, fighting tears at the thought of Miracle claiming her as a sister.

Miracle's face softened slightly, and the corners of her mouth turned up into a small smile. "You are one of us, Emery. Family. And Channings protect our own."

"Yes, they do," Knox agreed gruffly. Letting go of her, he walked over to Miracle and lifted a hand, gently caressing her face. "Fine. You can be a part of this,

Miracle, but you need to be vigilant. We cannot afford to lose you again."

Miracle nodded, leaning into his touch, before turning to walk away.

"Does she know how to use those guns?" Emery whispered, watching Miracle walk into a room at the end of the hall.

"I trained her myself," Briar said quietly, looping an arm through Emery's. "I don't ever want her to feel helpless like she did before."

As Knox's brothers all followed him down the hall after Miracle, Emery looked at Briar. "And you? Where did you learn to shoot a gun?"

Briar smiled, but it didn't reach her eyes. They were hard as steel as she replied, "My father taught all of us how to handle a weapon when we were growing up. He raised us to always try to combat confrontation with words first. If that doesn't work, we will do whatever it takes to protect our family."

"I hate bringing a war to your door."

"Emery," Knox interrupted, walking toward them, a wicked looking gun in his hand, "do you know how to use one of these?"

Emery nodded, slowly reaching out and taking the weapon from him. "Just point and shoot."

"Emery..."

"My father took me hunting with him a few times. We used a rifle, but this can't be much different."

She listened intently while her mate explained the 9mm handgun to her. The others returned as he was securing it at her waist, and she grasped his hand tightly when he was done, looking at them all. "You don't know what this means to me," she whispered. "My father was the only one who ever really cared about me. My mother and my brothers, they've never wanted anything to do with me. I didn't know what it was like to have a family, a real family, until I met you. I just want you to know that I love all of you very much, and I am so grateful for each and every one of you."

"We love you, too," Brayden said, reaching out to tug on her hair lightly. "Now, let's go make sure you never have to worry about your brothers, or that piece of shit alpha, again."

Moisture filled her eyes, but Emery refused to let the tears fall. They were standing strong for her, and she would do the same. "Yes, let's go."

TWENTY-ONE

K nox stood tall beside his mate, waiting for the convoy of vehicles that had just turned down the driveway to reach him. Briar stood next to him, Noah beside her, and Brayden was on the other side of Emery. Nolan and Miracle were hidden, one in the hayloft, and one on the roof of the house, their rifles pointed in the direction of the trucks. The sun was just going down, but the flood lights were on. He wanted to make sure he could look the bastard of an alpha in the eye when he gutted him for threatening his bunny.

"Were you really going to start all the fun without us?"

A slow grin crossed his face, but Knox's gaze didn't waiver from the scene in front of him. "Nice to have you here, Aurora."

He was aware of her walking out of the woods behind the barn, and she was not alone. She'd brought her coven, just as she'd said she would.

"I didn't want you to have all the fun," she

murmured, as she came to a stop by Noah. "Hey fur ball. Miss me?"

A deep growl rumbled in Noah's throat, but he didn't respond. Their mating was not going to be an easy one, if it happened at all. It was hard to fight a mate bond, but with the way Noah felt about witches, Knox knew he would deny it for as long as possible.

The first SUV came to a stop in front of them, as more witches emerged from the trees and fanned out around them. Knox didn't really give a damn how Noah felt about the women, he was glad to have them on their side.

"That's Samson," Emery said quietly, as the driver's side door opened, and a tall, muscular man appeared. Three more men stepped out. "The one on the left is Dryden, Samson's head enforcer. The other two are my brothers, Frederick and Hamilton."

Knox watched as the other three vehicles stopped. Four men and a woman emerged from the second one, three men from the third one, and four men from the last one.

"This isn't all of them," Aurora said, making a motion behind her with a hand that sent four of the witches back into the woods. "They brought backup. Coyotes."

Noah swore softly. "How many?"

"I'm not sure," Aurora admitted. "I just know they are there."

Knox nodded, his eyes on Samson. "Your witches have a way of checking back in once they find out?"

"Yes."

"Knox," Emery interjected, and he could hear the

worry in her voice, "that's Meadow. Why would he bring her to something like this?"

"Because he knows that she helped you escape," Aurora said softly. "He is going to make an example of her."

"Like hell, he is," Briar snapped.

"Agreed," Knox muttered.

Samson stepped forward, coming to a stop a few feet in front of Knox and Emery, a cruel grin pasted on his face. "Hello, Princess. Time to come home."

"I'm not going anywhere with you," Emery replied, not moving.

"Your mate is waiting," her brother said, motioning to where Alpha Ramsey stood next to Frederick and Hamilton, a frightened Meadow by his side.

"That asshat is *not* my mate."

"Not yet, but he will be soon."

"Emery is mine," Knox growled. "We have already completed the mate bond. If you take one step closer to her, you and all of your men will die."

"You promised her to me!" Alpha Ramsey snarled, dark anger flowing from him as he grabbed Meadow by her hair and threw her roughly to the ground in front of him. "This is your fault, daughter!"

Knox expected the young woman to cower in front of the asshole, or to try to run from him, but she did neither. Slowly, she rose to her feet, squared her shoulders, and said, "It's over, Father. Emery has made her choice. You can't break a mate bond once it's in place."

"You little bitch!" Curling his hand into a fist, the

alpha swung, connecting with Meadow's jaw, dropping her back to the ground. "Kill her!"

"I wouldn't do that if I were you," Knox said calmly, a cold grin on his face as he stared at Ramsey's enforcer who had pulled his gun from its holster. "My brother has a bead on you right now. If you even point that gun at her, you're a dead man."

"Do it!" Ramsey snarled.

"Did I forget to mention that my sister has her gun pointed directly at your head, Alpha?" Knox didn't wait for a response. "Meadow, come to us. You are safe." When she hesitated, he promised, "We have you covered. There is nothing he can do to you."

Slowly, she stumbled to her feet, taking a tentative step in his direction. Suddenly, a loud crack filled the air, and Ramsey's enforcer fell to the ground, his gun at his side. Knox raised an eyebrow, his gaze on Ramsey. "I warned you what would happen if your puppet raised his gun. You are on my property, Alpha Ramsey, in a territory that doesn't belong to you. I suggest you vacate the premises, without your daughter, if you want to live."

"We aren't alone," Samson snarled, taking a step in their direction.

"Neither are we," Knox promised, satisfaction filling him when low growls sounded around him, and several lions began to appear, slinking in from the woods, surrounding all of them. A large, golden lion with a large patch of black on his right shoulder came to a stop beside him, and Knox nodded, recognizing Garrith. "Did I mention this isn't your territory? Leo Lyouns is the alpha here. This is his son, Garrith, and these are his lions.

Looks like you forgot to check in when you arrived. They really hate that."

"Fuck you!"

"Meadow, come here. I promise, we will protect you."

Knox watched as a spark of hope flared in the young woman's eyes, and she didn't look back as she ran to him, slipping behind his back as if to hide from her father. "Thank you."

"Meadow, get your ass back over here," Ramsey growled, taking a step toward them. A shot rang out, kicking up dirt at the alpha's feet. He jumped back quickly, glaring at them.

"I warned you," Knox said calmly, his eyes on Samson now. "That was just a warning shot. The next one will go through your head."

"Fuck this shit," Ramsey snarled, motioning to his SUV. "You're on your own, Samson. Your sister isn't worth it."

The moment the words left his mouth, Knox knew something was up. There was no way Ramsey had come all of the way to Moonstone for Emery, just to turn tail and run. "He's bluffing," he warned the others, just as the man dropped to the ground and one of his enforcers pulled a gun, aiming at Noah and pulling the trigger.

CHAPTER
TWENTY-TWO

Emery's eyes flew to Noah in horror, expecting the bullet to hit him, but it never happened. It seemed to bounce off an invisible shield, falling harmlessly to the ground.

"Witches!" Samson spat, a gun appearing in his hand.

"Damn right!" Aurora hollered, and Emery watched in shock when her friend held up her hand and a ball of flames began to form. "Let me show you what happens when you fuck with my friend," she spat, before letting it fly. It hit the enforcer who shot at Noah, engulfing him in flames.

All hell broke loose after that. Gunfire filled the air, and Emery raised her own weapon, feeling the kick of the gun in her hand when the bullet left the chamber.

"Get in the barn!" Knox snarled, taking her arm and pushing her away from him. "Get Meadow out of here!"

"My people found the coyotes!" Aurora yelled, another ball of flames leaving her hand. "They took out as many as they could, but the rest will be here anytime."

No sooner did the words leave her lips, then several coyotes flooded from the trees. The lions turned to face them, waiting until they were only a few feet away, before attacking.

It was a sight to see, but there was no way in hell Emery was sticking around to watch the outcome. She was a bunny, for fucks sake! She wouldn't stand a chance with all of those huge teeth and claws. Grabbing Meadow's arm, she yelled, "Let's go! We need to get you somewhere safe!"

She and Meadow had just about reached the barn door when two coyotes slunk over to block the entrance. They growled, their fangs dripping with saliva, as they crouched low. Emery raised her gun, intent on protecting Meadow, when a loud roar split the air. Sidetracked for a moment, she almost missed it when the coyote sprang at her. Pulling the trigger, she cried out when the bullet hit its target, dropping him to the ground. Before she could point the weapon at the other coyote, a large blur rushed past her, swiping at the downed coyote on the way, sending it flying into the side of the barn. The other one tried to retreat, but the massive beast in front of her was having none of that. He sank his huge claws deep into his prey, tearing it apart, piece-by-piece, not stopping until there was nothing left. When it was finished, he turned to look at her, letting out another loud roar, but Emery wasn't afraid.

Rushing forward, she hugged him quickly before leaning back to smack a smooch on his snout. "Thank you, my love! Now, go help the others! I'm going up with Miracle."

With one last look at her, he left, barreling back into the fight.

"Oh, my God!" Meadow cried, her shocked gaze on the vicious fighting going on around them. "Why is this happening, Princess? Why?"

"Let's go!" Grabbing her arm again, Emery urged her into the barn and up a ladder in the back. She found Miracle on her belly up in the hayloft by the partially open door, methodically pulling the trigger as she picked off bad guys. "Miracle, this is horrible. It needs to stop!"

"Don't worry," she said, as she pulled the trigger again. "It will all be over soon."

"So much death and destruction because of me," Emery cried, tears now streaming down her face. "I have to end this."

"No, the death and destruction is because your brothers are fucking idiots," Miracle snarled, the rifle kicking in her hands again. "None of this is on you, Emery."

"If I had just left, this wouldn't be happening right now."

"If you had left, I would have tracked you down myself," Miracle replied, repositioning the gun and firing again. "We are your family, Emery. We love you, and we need you here with us. Knox needs you."

Emery nodded, stiffening when there was a sound at the back of the loft. Turning, she shoved Meadow behind her, raising her gun.

"You wouldn't shoot your own brother, would you,

Princess?" Samson asked, his eyes narrowing on her. "We're family."

"Did you not just hear what I said, douchebag?" Miracle asked, swinging around, her rifle in her hands. "Emery is *our* family now."

"Never," Samson growled, his revolver trained on Miracle. "I'm taking her home with me. She's going to mate with Alpha Ramsey, and I'm getting my fucking money I was promised."

"Dream on."

Before Miracle could fire, there was a muffled shot, and a large red stain appeared in the middle of Samson's chest. His eyes widened in shock, as he looked down, dropping his gun.

"That's where you are wrong, asshole. Princess is staying right here, where she is happy and loved. Something she never got at home. You aren't going to hurt her anymore."

Emery's eyes widened, and she took a step forward. "Dryden?"

Dryden didn't respond as he put a bullet in between Samson's eyes. Her brother slowly collapsed to the floor, staring lifelessly at the ceiling.

When Dryden finally raised his gaze to meet hers, Emery whispered, "Thank you."

"I failed you before, Princess. I knew Ramsey was a prick, but I thought I needed to follow your brother like I did your father. Be loyal to him and do as he commanded. I was wrong. I will never be able to make up for that."

"You just did," Emery said, aware that Miracle was

123

once again looking out the door to the hayloft. It was a lot quieter now, the gunfire fading into the background. The snarls and growls were lessening, and hope began to fill her. "Is it over?"

Miracle turned back, a small grin on her face. "Yes, I think it is."

Emery crossed the floor to look out, tears filling her eyes at all of the carnage below. So many hurt, and several dead, all because of her.

"You have to stop thinking like that," Miracle said softly, rising to stand beside her, slipping an arm around her waist to hold her close. "None of this is your fault. The blame falls solely on your brothers."

"And Lela," Dryden added, derision in his voice. "That woman is not without blame."

"I just don't understand what I did to make them hate me so much," Emery whispered. "Why would they want to sell me off like that?"

"I can answer that," Dryden told her, "but right now, I think we better get down there and help the wounded."

"Yes! Of course!"

Upset with herself for not immediately going to check on the others, Emery left the hayloft, clearing the stairs quickly, and running for the door.

"Princess! Dammit, Princess, wait! I need to make sure it's safe first."

Several growls filled the air when Dryden's hand circled around the upper part of her arm, and the huge barn seemed awful small when they were suddenly surrounded by three large bears, their teeth bared as they stared at Dryden.

"Stop!" Emery demanded, stomping her foot to get their attention. "Stop, you guys! He isn't going to hurt me. He saved my life." When the growling continued, she snapped, "He just put a bullet in Samson's head to protect me. Do you really think he is going to hurt me now?"

The growling slowly subsided, and then there was a soft, shimmering light around the largest bear as he began to shift. Soon, Knox was standing in front of her, in all his naked glory, his eyes on Dryden. "Thank you for saving my mate's life."

Dryden bowed his head low, tilting it to the side in deference to Knox, "I am only sorry I didn't do anything sooner."

"Me, too," Briar snapped, striding over to them. "Then we wouldn't have had to just kick a bunch of bunny and coyote butt! Knox, we have several injured people here, on both sides."

"My other brothers?" Emery whispered, looking toward the door.

"They are both dead," Knox growled, sliding his arms around her and pulling her close. "They will never hurt you again."

"And, my father?" Meadow asked quietly.

"I'm sorry, Meadow. Alpha Ramsey slipped away with one of his goons in the middle of the fight. But, you are going to stay here with us. You're safe now."

Meadow shook her head, wrapping her arms tightly around her waist. "I will never be safe while he is still on this earth."

Emery slipped away from Knox and went to her. "Meadow, you can trust my mate and his family."

Meadow sighed, "It has nothing to do with trust, Princess. I just know that my father will never let me go."

"He was going to have one of his men kill you," Briar said, raising an eyebrow. "Why would he care where you are at this point?"

"Just because he doesn't want me, doesn't mean he will let you have me," Meadow said softly. "He will either find a way to get me back, or have me taken out."

"Taken out?" Emery cringed at the woman's choice of words.

"That's what he calls it when he places a hit on someone."

"Does he do that often?" Knox asked, accepting a pair of jogging pants Miracle handed him. He'd told Emery once that they kept several pairs of pants around the ranch, because you never know when you would need them after a shift. She was glad, because none of the females outside the barn needed to see her mate's dick. Hell, none of them *in* the barn needed to, related or not.

"Yes," came the soft, honest reply. "He says it is his way of dispensing justice on those who have wronged him."

"It looks like all of the survivors who were able to, have left the area," Garrith said, as he entered the barn, interrupting their conversation. "The ones that are left are going to be handed over to the local sheriff after they've been treated for their injuries."

"Is that wise?" Dryden asked. "Do you really want to

hand shifters over to humans, whether they know about us or not?"

"Who says he's human?" Garrith asked, before turning to saunter away. Pausing, he looked back, "By the way, my mom is expecting you all over for dinner on Sunday. I suggest you be there."

"Shit," Briar muttered, shaking her head after he left. "The last time I ran into that woman, she tried to set me up with one of her mangy lions."

A slow smile appeared on Emery's lips as she looked up at her mate.

"What is it, baby?"

"I'm free," she whispered, her smile growing wider. "Well, unless that douche canoe Ramsey comes back for me."

"He won't be back for you," Meadow said. "He will focus on me now."

"Not for a while," Aurora promised, appearing out of nowhere. "He is going to need time to regroup."

"Aurora!" Meadow flew to the witch, falling into her arms, holding her tightly as she sobbed. "I can't believe you're here."

"I see you are finally ready to be free of that bastard," Aurora said softly, gently patting her back. "I'm so glad, my friend."

Meadow leaned back, and whispered, "I am, but there is one more thing I have to do."

Aurora nodded slowly, "I see. Well, we will get it handled after everything here is settled."

"Thank you."

"I don't even want to know what the fuck you two are talking about," Noah snarled, shaking his head.

"We can worry about that later," Knox interjected, and Emery sighed when he tugged her close again, wrapping her in his arms. "Right now, we need to give the injured who are still here medical attention, and then get this place cleaned up."

"Cleaned up? You mean you need to dispose of the bodies?" Emery asked quietly.

"That's not for you to worry about, baby," Knox said, kissing her gently. "I'll handle it."

"Aurora."

Emery turned to look at the people who stood off to the side, waiting patiently. It was Aurora's coven, all eight of them, all females, and all with very distinct features and abilities. Some of those abilities she'd seen for herself. "Thank you," she whispered, leaving Knox's arms once again, so that she could go give each of them a hug. "Thank you all so much for coming to Moonstone to help me. You will never know how much it means to me."

"Yes," one of them said softly, a sweet smile on her face, "we do. And you are very welcome."

"We must go now," one of the others said, a worried look on her face. "I need to get back to my charge."

"Charge?"

"It's what I call the person I'm trying to keep safe. This assignment is proving to be rather difficult."

"If you need help, Mist, all you have to do is ask," Aurora said. "I would be more than happy to return the favor after everything you did for me today."

The other woman's arresting grey eyes softened, and she nodded, "Thank you, sister."

Emery watched them leave, before turning to Aurora. "You better get Meadow out of here, just in case local law enforcement shows up. You can bring her back later tonight. We will have a room ready."

"No, thank you," Meadow murmured. "Thank you for everything you have done for me, but I am going to stay with Aurora."

Emery nodded, knowing it was better not to argue. Meadow had known Aurora for a long time, and she trusted her. That's where she needed to be. "Be safe. Both of you."

"I'm going to leave now, too, if that is acceptable, Princess." Dryden cut in. "I have things to take care of back home with the herd."

"Emery."

"What?"

"My name is Emery now. It suits me better than Princess."

Dryden smiled, bowing slightly. "I like it."

"Dryden, before you go, will you answer a question for me?" When he paused, she asked, "Did my brothers have my father killed?"

Dryden stiffened, looking off into the distance for a moment before answering, "I wasn't there that night, but I've always had my suspicions."

"Which are?" she prompted when he hesitated.

"I think Samson made a deal with Alpha Ramsey, and your other brothers backed him on it. Ramsey had his coyote buddies kill your father, and then Samson would sell him you when he was out of the picture."

"But, all he would have gained out of the deal is a mating with Emery," Briar said, tilting her head to the side as she looked at them. "Why would he pay so much just for a mate?" As an afterthought, she looked at Emery, "Sorry, sis. I didn't mean anything by that."

"I have learned over the past few months that Alpha Ramsey is one crafty son of a bitch. I think his plan was to mate with Emery, then kill Samson and take over the herd, merging it with his. With Emery as his mate, it wouldn't have been a difficult transition for everyone."

"Except none of our herd is loyal to me," Emery said, shaking her head. "They were only loyal to my mother and brothers."

"No, they were scared of Lela and your brothers. There's a difference. Emery, there is something you need to know. Lela is not your real mother. I don't like to be the one to tell you this, but your father slept with one of the women in the herd. She passed away in childbirth, and he moved you in with him, commanding Lela to act as if you were her own child. She always resented that."

"Oh!" Emery gasped in horror, her hand going up to cover her mouth. No wonder her mother had never loved her. "I had no idea."

"He didn't want you to," Dryden said gently. "He forbade everyone in the herd from talking about it. The punishment was death."

"Damn."

Emery heard the soft curse from Briar, but her mind

was spinning with everything she'd just been told. She didn't think she could handle much more. "Knox."

"I'm right here, baby."

She felt herself being lifted into his arms, and then he was striding away from everyone as he called over his shoulder, "Dryden, go tend to your herd. Stay the fuck out of Moonstone unless you ask permission from the town's alpha first."

Dryden's response was lost to her. Her thoughts were on how her brothers' betrayal, and the fact that the woman she'd called mother all her life wasn't her mother after all.

They made it into the house and up to their bedroom before the first tear fell. Knox quickly stripped her clothes off, leaving her in just her underwear, before slipping one of his shirts over her head. Then he was holding her close as they lay in bed, her tears soaking his chest.

"It's going to be okay, sweet bunny," he told her, running his hands up and down her back. "It's all going to be okay."

CHAPTER
TWENTY-THREE

Emery woke to the sound of soft snores beneath her ear, and the scent of her mate surrounding her. Sliding her hand through the thick patch of hair on Knox's chest, she sighed as she rubbed her cheek against it. Damn, she loved this man.

Turning her head, she slowly licked at his nipple, before sucking it into her mouth and nibbling on it with her teeth. Her hand slipped down his chest, over his hard abs, and under the waistband of his jogging pants, grasping the already thickening cock below. She began to slowly stroke him, as she licked her way down his front, intent on finding what those pants were hiding.

"Fuck, baby," he groaned, reaching down quickly to slide them over his hips, freeing his dick, and then past his thighs and pushing them away.

"Mine," she whispered, trailing hot, wet kisses over his stomach, following the treasure trail of hair down to the thick cock that rose to attention, waiting for her mouth.

"Yours!" he agreed, lifting his hips as if to hurry her along.

"Patience," she whispered, licking and sucking her way down lower, teasing each tantalizing inch of his skin with her tongue.

"Fuck that," he snarled, sliding his fingers into her hair and gripping tightly as he guided her to his dick.

Emery moaned at the sight of pre-cum that beaded up at the tip of his cock, then spilled over to slip down the side. "Mine!" she growled, catching it with her tongue, and licking all of the way up until she swirled her tongue around the tip to make sure she got it all. Teasing him, she slowly ran her tongue back down his length, and then up the other side.

Tightening his grip in her hair, Knox held her still and pushed into the hot cavern of her mouth. When she tried to pull away, he groaned, "Please baby. I want to fuck your mouth. It feels so good."

Well, since he put it that way... Emery paused, waiting for him to take over. She didn't have to wait long. At first, he guided her head up and down, her mouth slick and wet on his cock. She sucked him deep, loving the noises he made, making her grind against his leg seeking her own pleasure.

"Baby, I need to be inside you." That's what he said, but instead he held her still and began to thrust deep into her mouth, slow at first, and then faster and faster.

Reaching down, she quickly slid off her panties. Her hand went between her legs, two fingers inside her pussy, then back out to circle around her clit. The entire time, her mate pushed into her mouth, groaning her name over and over.

All of a sudden, Knox pulled from her mouth, and growled, "I want inside you. Now."

Before she could blink, she was on all fours, and he was behind her, low growls rumbling throughout the room. He pushed down on her shoulders, until her upper half was low on the bed, and her ass was high in the air. Running a hand over her round globes, he snarled, "Fucking gorgeous."

Emery cried out when he grasped one hip firmly, and guided his cock inside her, stretching her, filling her. He began to move, not bothering with a slow pace. He thrust deep, hard, and fast, his claws emerging and digging into her sides. She clutched the wooden slats on the headboard, pushing back into him, her screams filling the room. He was wild, out of control with a hint of desperation, and she loved it.

Her orgasm rose fast, and soon she was tumbling over the edge, with him following. He sank his fangs deep into her shoulder, stiffening as he came inside her.

They stayed like that for several minutes, before Knox finally removed his teeth and collapsed on the bed, holding her close to him. He trailed kisses over her face, his hand sliding up and down her back. "You're safe now, sweet bunny," he rasped, burying his head into her shoulder. "No one is ever going to hurt you again. I promise."

Emery rolled over, cupping his face in her hand as she whispered, "I know."

"You do?"

"Hell, yeah!" Emery said with a grin. "My bear will eat anyone who tries to. And, not in a good way!"

Knox threw his head back and laughed, before capturing her lips with his. Then, he slowly started to slide down her body. "No, I save that for my bunny."

Her eyes widened, and then she reached up to grasp the headboard again as he proceeded to show her just how much her bear liked to eat his bunny.

Make sure and visit my website for information on all of my books, and to sign up for my Newsletter where you will receive all of the latest information on new releases, sales, and more!

https://www.dawnsullivanauthor.com/

I would love to have you join my reader's group, Author Dawn Sullivan's Rebel Readers, so that we can hang out and chat, and where you will also get sneak peeks of cover reveals, read excerpts before anyone else, and more!

https://www.facebook.com/groups/
AuthorDawnSullivansRebelReaders/

About the Author

Dawn Sullivan has a wonderful, supportive husband, and three beautiful children. She enjoys spending time with them, which normally involves some baseball, shooting hoops, taking walks, watching movies, and reading.

Her passion for reading began at a very young age and only grew over time. Whether she was bringing home a book from the library or sneaking one of her mother's romance novels to read by the light in the hallway when she was supposed to be sleeping, Dawn always had a book. She reads several different genres and subgenres, but Paranormal Romance and Romantic Suspense are her favorites.

Dawn has always made up stories of her own, and finally decided to start sharing them with others. She hopes everyone enjoys reading them as much as she enjoys writing them.

OTHER BOOKS BY DAWN SULLIVAN

Sass and Growl

Book 1 His Bunny Kicks Sass

Book 2 Protecting His Fox's Sass

Book 3 Accepting His Witch's Sass

Book 4 Chasing His Lynx's Sass

Chosen By Destiny

Book 1 Blayke

Book 2 Bellame

Alluring Assassins

Book 1 Cassia

Dark Leopards East Texas Chapter- this series is written with three other authors

Book 1 Shadow's Revenge

Book 7 Demon's Hellfire

Book 10 Taz's Valor

Magical Mojo

Book 1 Witch Way To Love

Book 2 Witch Way To Jingle

Book 3 Witch Way To Cupid

Rogue Enforcers

Karma

Alayla

Made in the USA
Columbia, SC
31 January 2025